Tony Bury, born in 1972 in Northampton, England, has had a passion for writing songs, poems and short stories since an early age. He has taken it more seriously since having kids, writing several children's books and screen plays as well as the Alex Keaton series of crime novels and the Edmund Carson series.

DARKNESS FALLS

Also by Tony Bury

The Alex Keaton Series:

Intervention Forgiven
Intervention Needed
The Intervention

The Edmund Carson Series:
Inside Edmund Carson

Tony Bury

DARKNESS FALLS

Vanguard Press

A CIP catalogue record for this title is
available from the British Library.

ISBN 978 1 784652 85 2

Vanguard Press is an imprint of
Pegasus Elliot MacKenzie Publishers Ltd.
www.pegasuspublishers.com

First Published in 2017

Vanguard Press
Sheraton House Castle Park
Cambridge England

Printed & Bound in Great Britain

For those who lost their battle with darkness. R.I.P.

Chapter 1

She could just about make out in the darkness that either side of the alleyway was covered in empty boxes and rubbish bins. There was a faint light in the distance, the light was not strong enough to make out what was at the end. She had no choice but to continue to walk through. Something was pulling her forward. The boxes rustled with what she hoped were mice or rats scavenging for food. She watched them carefully nonetheless. Not wanting a surprise jumping out at her as she walked. She could feel her heart beating faster as she did. There was a surge in her veins, she could feel the blood as it pumped through her body. It was hot and throbbing.

Smoke was coming up from the vents under her feet, she presumed these were underground kitchens. There was a rustle of pots and pans and a language that she recognised, all those takeaways had taught her the sound of Chinese.

It was cold, her breath was in front of her as she walked. The door to her right burst open which made her jump back. A Chinese man threw a pot of water out five steps in front of her. He was still talking to an unknown person inside as he did, he didn't see her, and returned as if she wasn't there. She continued walking, the end of the alleyway wasn't getting closer. The light remained the same distance in front of her at all times.

The door to her left swung open. She froze. Holding her breath as she waited but nothing came out. She knew she was destined to go inside. As soon as she did, she could smell blood, it was as familiar as fresh bread to her by now. The door led her into a deserted warehouse. Placed in the far right corner of the floor was a single bed. Other than this, there was nothing in the warehouse. She slowly began to walk closer, carefully looking around her as she did. The blood was coming from somewhere. She could smell it.

On the bed was an unknown person. Dressed in trousers and a jacket, over their head someone had placed a hood. At the end of the bed a file. She picked up the file. Picture after picture of murder victims. It was the pictures, they smelled of the blood, each one of them. The scent was strong, overpowering, this person's file was drowning in blood. There were names and paper cuttings of each of the victims. On the front of the file was a number but it kept changing, it was an ever increasing clock. The file was thick and weighed heavily in her hands, getting heavier every second. She dropped it on the bed. Some of the pictures fell to the floor as she did. She stood looking at them. Blood started to trickle out of them. They were familiar; she didn't know why but she knew these people. She left them where they lay. Whoever this was, it was a bad person. This was one of them, one of the Brown Institute people. They needed to die. All her instincts knew that to be true. She didn't need to read the file to tell her that.

She moved her hand to her side to feel for her gun. It wasn't there. For a moment there was a feeling of panic. She then placed her hand behind her back and grabbed at a knife that was placed in the back of her jeans. As she took it out, there was a flash of light from the street outside. It reflected off the steel and the golden lion-headed handle. It took her back for a second. Memories were flooding her mind. There was a girl. A dark hood. And this knife, this knife was familiar. Was this who was laying on the bed? This girl? She didn't deserve to die? She was an innocent, she was sure of it.

This wasn't her. This was one of them. Everything in her body told her that. The person on the bed had to die. With one hand she lifted the knife above her head and with the other leaned over and pulled at the hood. The hood came off easily. Laying in front of her with her mouth bound and a cut across her cheek was Alex Keaton. Alex Keaton, the sight was a familiar one for her. She couldn't work out why. The file, the pictures, they were all of her kills. She froze, Alex was fighting on the bed to get up. She held the knife higher, to give more force. As her hand rose so did her head, she caught a glimpse of herself in the window.

Michael Mellor! The reflection was Michael Mellor. The knife came down with force directly at Alex…

"Arrrrgggggghhhhhh!" Alex screamed as if a knife had just pierced her skin.

"It's okay, it's okay. It was just a dream, Alex, just a dream." Oliver was above Alex and holding her shoulders to calm her down. He had been lying next to her all night, and become all too used to the night terrors. They were three, sometimes four, times a night when they were at their worst. Alex didn't sleep much on those nights. Neither did Oliver.

Alex was sweating and shaking with fear. Oliver managed to calm her down. She sat up in bed, and drank from the glass next to her.

"Michael?" Oliver didn't really need to ask, the worst dreams always had Michael in there somewhere. He had seeped into Alex's brain and wasn't letting go. Alex nodded. She laid back down. As she did she caught sight of the clock, it was nearly seven a.m. There was no trying to sleep again today. This was a blessing and a curse. Her sleep patterns had become more erratic than the months after her partner Paul Simpson had died. Before Alex had even heard of the Brown Institute Alex could feel it. The lack of sleep had her feeling more drained every day. Something had taken over Alex. It was taking everything she had to resist what felt like the inevitable cure. There was a way to have peace, but it came at a price.

Since the altercation with Stephen Henderson and Christopher Mellor, Alex knew the truth about what had happened to her. She knew that they had changed her in the Brown Institute and she could feel the DNA surging through her veins. They had implanted the cocktail of murderer into her body. Christopher Mellor had ensured that was all. His experiment was to create a murderer he could control. Someone who would help him clear up some of the previous patients. It had worked up until the point that Alex murdered him.

There was silence for the next thirty minutes. Alex and Oliver lay together, neither of them talking, just holding each other as they did. Alex watched the clock as each minute ticked over. As if something was going to change. It wasn't. The time just kept rolling on as they lay there.

"I don't think I can hold on much longer. I think I need a case." Oliver knew those words were coming at some point. When Alex was working she was better, calmer. After she had taken care of a case, there were even a few nights without dreams. Nights when she was at peace. Taking a life was the cost for a good night's sleep.

It had been a couple of weeks since the last case. That was too long. Oliver knew he had left it too long this time. Alex had been suffering for nights. They both understood the risk for them to take a case. They knew that the Mellors, the secret service and the police would all be looking for them. Cases were a clear beacon for anyone watching to come and track them down.

"I know. Don't worry, I have one. I have been tracking him for a while now." Oliver had taken over responsibility for the list and the tracker. He couldn't trust Alex with them, knowing what they had done to her. He was doing his best to keep them both safe. Alex sat up. Her eyes widened at the thought of work, she needed this. This was how she was surviving every day.

It had been three months since the fire at the Henderson house. Oliver and Alex had created as much distance as possible between them and the Whitehouse. Heading to Los Angeles, and then up to San Francisco. They were staying in a town just outside called Burlingame. It was a thirty-five-minute car journey to Fisherman's Wharf and the centre of San Francisco. Being close to a major city made them more at ease.

The bigger the population, the easier they would find it to disappear.

They had sold Alex's SUV that she bought in New York. They had sold a further five SUV's and a couple of houses worth of TVs, furniture and jewellery. Anything they could buy and sell on as soon as possible for a marked-down price, but always for cash buyers. They spent almost the whole first month trading. They had used the ATM daily but it had a three thousand dollars a day limit, and there was no telling how much cash they were going to need. Oliver and Alex knew they needed to get as much cash as possible out of the card before Maria was going to have it stopped. Maria was too busy grieving to even notice the card activity. It was hardly going to cause a ripple in the Mellor billions. It had been the Mellors' accountant speaking to Maria's mother Carly that had pointed out the other Black Card was still in use. He knew the card had been given to Miss Keaton. Carly just told him to cancel it. The card had now been cancelled for two weeks. Oliver had been to a bank in L.A. and the card was taken. They moved onto Burlingame that day. Alex and Oliver had enough money now to last them. Although they weren't living the high life they once were at the Waldorf Astoria. It had been motels and bed and breakfasts, always paying in cash as not to be noticed by anyone. Alex and Oliver were learning how to live outside the eyes of the law, or anyone else who was watching. They still had people looking for them. This wasn't over. If not the Mellors, certainly the board from the Brown Institute would be hunting them. Given what they were doing, the police also had a task force tracking them down. There was also the possibility Victoria Owens, the president of the United States, had the secret service looking for them. For the murder of Christopher Mellor, Stephen Henderson, their bodyguards and the woman who Stephen had abducted that evening, before Alex had arrived at the house. Nobody was going to know that Stephen Henderson was intending to kill her that night before Alex arrived.

Alex hadn't told Oliver about Dee. He wasn't aware that she had sent Dee Quaid to meet with the president should anything happen to her. The fact that the news reports had mentioned an unknown woman in the fire. She was convinced that Dee would have carried out her wishes. The president would now know of the Brown Institute, and Christopher Mellor's involvement in it. Oliver didn't need the added pressure of this and looking after Alex. Alex wanted to keep this secret.

Oliver still had secrets too. Ones he wasn't ready to share with Alex. They just needed to keep going for now, and to stay unseen from any eyes. But Alex, Alex above everything else needed to work.

"You have a case? Who is it?" Alex was surprised. Happy but surprised. The distance between cases made her feel like she was in and out of reality. She hadn't noticed Oliver working in the background. Oliver moved off the bed and walked across to his laptop that was over by the dresser.

"The guy's name is Victor. Victor Heller. He is a local gangster by all accounts. At least that is what he pretends to be. He comes from a well-to-do family, but decided to take to a life of crime. Rather than spend Mummy and Daddy's money." Alex was awake and alert all of a sudden, the thought of a case had her heart pumping again for the right reasons.

She had a flashback to her dream, it was the same feeling. The same feeling in her blood.

"It is not going to be easy, Alex, as he has quite the entourage. Every picture I can find of this guy he is surrounded with protection."

As the words came out of Oliver's mouth he knew that it wasn't going to be a problem. Alex didn't want easy. He didn't want easy for her. Over the past three months he could tell, the harder the case the more at ease Alex would be for the short while afterwards.

Over the time Oliver had been supporting Alex he had fallen in love with her. This had started from the first day he was assigned to her by Christopher Mellor. He had fought it at first as he was a professional. Alex's actions in the field, her character and everything she wanted to achieve, drew him to her. Everything that she had done, it didn't matter to him. He knew it was all for the right reasons. She had been operating outside of the law, but only to clear up a mess that he somehow felt some responsibility for. His time working for the Mellors and now seeing the monsters that they had created made him want to support Alex, no matter what.

"He spends most of his days around Fisherman's Wharf. I have been watching him. He has an apartment, sorry, an apartment block overlooking it. He and his family have a lot of property. This is just one of their places. I thought we could go there for lunch today and stake it out for a while?"

Alex nodded at Oliver and then headed to the bathroom. As she got to the door she gave a glance back at him as he sat on the bed. Oliver could hear the shower start. He followed after her. Oliver was thankful that there was one other thing that gave Alex peace for a short while. Something that gave them both peace.

After the shower they returned back to bed. Oliver sat watching the news and Alex started on the background of Victor Heller. Reading everything that Oliver had pulled together already and trawling the Internet for all the information she could. Victor had indeed been born to a well-to-do family. This wasn't a surprise to her. Probably another recommendation by Christopher Mellor. Not that he would be doing that again. The Hellers were big in property in San Francisco. Made their fortune mainly in commercial properties but dabbled in the housing market. Victor, however, chose a different profession. Drugs, prostitution and violence. The violence had seen him do a few episodes in prison. But nothing more than six months at a time. There were strong reports that some of his men had been involved in at least a dozen murder cases. So far nothing linked back to him. He had been careful in how he dealt with business. He was a highly educated man, who by all accounts was acting out to his parents.

She knew what he was. He was a Brown Institute baby. Although Alex hadn't been born at the Institute, she now knew what that felt like too. Whatever had happened historically with these murders, she knew that Victor would have been knee deep in it. She could feel it.

"How is the research going?" Oliver turned down the TV to talk to Alex. He had already done his homework but purposely hadn't included everything in his notes. Alex needed to work. She needed the focus.

"I think it is safe to say that he is not a nice man. I don't understand why he would have turned to this. He could have had anything he wanted." Alex knew the problem with those words as they came out.

"I guess I do understand the need. But you know what I mean. I am sure there were other ways he could have got his fix?" Alex was tying herself in knots with trying to separate herself from the other Brown Institute patients. Still coming to terms with the fact she was one of them. Part of her also struggled with the fact that if people had money, why would they hit the streets for this fix? Michael had been different. His father had controlled his dark side for him.

"There are four cases that have been linked to him for murder and another eight or so to members of his gang. Various reports on drugs and prostitutes. He has been inside a few times. I would guess that is where he found his friends. Money buys you good lawyers as he didn't stay there long?" Oliver had known all this already.

"So, I guess we are ready for lunch?" Oliver smiled at Alex. She was smiling back. Excitement of the case had her focused and ready for work.

"I am ready whenever you are." Oliver jumped off the bed and turned the TV off.

* * * *

"Gentlemen, gentlemen. Let me assure you that the Mellor Foundation will still be fully supporting the Institute's needs. My father understood the great work that we are doing here, and he understood the need for secrecy. As do I." Maria paused to make sure that she was looking all the board members directly in the eye. There had been a fear that with her father gone some of the board members would change their allegiances to the government or even the president. Maria was keen for that not to happen.

"As his only living heir I have made a decision to take on the vacant post of CEO. I will, as I pointed out in my report, be doing a thorough investigation into the business and its future needs." There was considerable mumbling from the boardroom. The board were eleven men in total. All old enough to be Maria's father or grandfather. They were captains of industry, property tycoons and men of serious wealth. The Mellors by far were the biggest single shareholder in their business. Christopher Mellor had led these people over the last two decades. Although lately he had started to fear the board unifying together against him. This room represented the real government of the country. They controlled everything from behind the scenes.

"If either of you would like to step down your position in protest of this, please feel free to do so. The door is always open. I am sure that we can survive without you."

The mumbling stopped. Maria meant that. The tone of her voice was similar to her father's now. She didn't fear them. But they were beginning to fear her. Which was the reaction that she had wanted. The board in the last two decades had two people resign. Both of which had met with an unfortunate accident within days of their resignation. It was never mentioned. They each knew that secrecy was paramount to the success of the country. And their ever growing empire. Anyone willing to leave could not be trusted.

Maria had just threatened them. They all understood this. She had just done it with a smile on her face. It was time for her to stand up and lead her father's business interests.

The research and technology that the Institutes were developing attributed to the fact that revenue was at an all-time high. Private investors and secret government bodies all wanted in on this work and were paying accordingly. Secrecy was key. Presidents and kings didn't know about the Institutes. But Generals, dictators and billionaires did. They were all in it for the money and the power this work would bring.

Ethics were not something they discussed on the board. They knew some of this work would end up in the wrong hands. Each board member was taking a high nine figure salary from the work they were doing. And none of them wanted this to stop. Maria understood that money talks.

"I will take your silence as complete support to my announcement and thank you for the continued support. We will call another meeting for a fortnight's time. By then I will have started my investigation. Then if there is nothing else, gentlemen. I suggest we have concluded our business for the day. You know your way out." Maria sat back in her chair at the head of the table. She picked up her phone and started to type. This was just to ensure that nobody spoke to her as they left. She wasn't interested in chit-chat.

In silence slowly the room cleared, leaving Maria alone. Maria breathed a sigh of relief. She had expected them to be stronger. Especially given she was a woman in a man's world. Her father always told her that people in business generally wanted to be led. So if you assume the role as leader they will fall into place. This was certainly the case today.

A few moments later James walked through the door.

"Your car is ready, madam."

"Stop calling me madam, James. You make me sound like my mother. Besides I am still in my thirties. A madam is like sixty. Or turning tricks with prostitutes for money. Come to think of it, considering who I was just in the room with? I may be a madam... How is the leg by the way? I have been meaning to ask."

"It's fine, mad...Miss Mellor."

"Mad Miss Mellor, is that what they are calling me now? I am not surprised. I quite like it though." Maria smiled at him.

"I have told you before, Maria is just fine, James. Good, I am glad to hear that, about your leg. You can barely tell you were shot." Maria paused, remembering the event. Alex shot James just before she killed her father at the Henderson house.

"Speaking of that, what of our other little problem? Do we have any updates on their whereabouts? I must say, they are becoming very good at this hide-and-seek game?"

"No, Maria. No news. They haven't been seen for a month now. They will have been long gone from L.A. now and have cash so they could be anywhere. Oliver is very well trained. If he doesn't want to be found, he won't be." Nearly every day James had been asked for an update on Alex and Oliver. It was the same answer. They were still untraceable.

"So I can tell. We need to find them, and deal with them, James. We can't have them running around on the loose. There is too much at stake. My father's little experiment is going to come back and bite us at some point if we don't deal with it." James could tell how worried she was about this.

"We need to ensure secrecy also. I don't want the board to get nervous about this. As far as they are concerned this matter has been dealt with." Maria spoke in a soft tone. Alex had been capable of so much in the short time of knowing her. Now she was partnered up with one of her father's most loyal employees. If they wanted to cause a scene, she had no doubt that they could.

"I understand, and it will be dealt with, Maria."

"I know, James. I know it must be hard for you as well, as he was your friend and your boss. Alex Keaton certainly has her appeal. Thank you. Okay. Is my blue suit in the back of the car? I can get changed in there."

"Yes, Maria, it is all there." Maria had packed up her laptop as she spoke and started to head towards the door.

"Good, then take me to the Whitehouse. I sense Victoria Owens has some questions that she would like answering."

* * * *

Oliver drove the thirty-five minutes to the Fisherman's Wharf. He parked close to the restaurants so that if a quick getaway was needed they would be prepared. From the wharf you could see Victor Heller's apartment building. He had been spending most of his time in there, Oliver figured it was his base of operations. He wasn't wrong. They managed to get a table outside a small sandwich shop facing the apartment block. Oliver went in, twenty minutes later returned, bringing out lunch.

"Think this place must be world-famous or something. The queue in there was unbelievable. Must be a hundred people. For a sandwich and some chips." Alex didn't respond. It had been far too long since her last case, and now there was one in sight. Her focus was only on the building. Oliver could see it in her eyes. This morning's playfulness in the shower and her smiles at her laptop had disappeared. She had fully changed into work mode. He placed the food in front of her and sat down to eat. The tracker showed that Victor was inside. The coming and goings of the building suggested that there were drugs involved to the trained eye. High traffic with a fast turnaround of people. Nobody else around seemed to notice. Oliver ate his food while Alex pushed hers around the basket. Oliver didn't expect her to eat. He knew once today was over her appetite for food would return. As would her appetite for life. Over the last three months he never pushed Alex to do anything. She was dealing with what had happened to her. He spent his time supporting and taking care of her.

"How many do you think are in there?" Oliver knew that question was coming. Her first thought was always how many they were going to have to take care of.

"I have been watching. Everyone that has gone in has come out again. Anywhere between five and fifteen minutes. There is no way of really knowing." The next question was predictable.

"Unless we go in? And make a purchase? It has to be drugs in there, doesn't it?" Alex was looking directly at Oliver now. There was a hunger in her eyes; Oliver could see it.

"We can't do that. We could be walking into a minefield. You know that, Alex. I suggest we do the next best thing and follow one of the people who does know what it is like in there. Ask them a few questions of our own?" Alex nodded her head at Oliver. She knew he was right. She was just feeling the urge to be in there and dealing with the case, it was so close. She knew she was craving the release that only taking a life was going to give her.

* * * *

James drove Maria to the Whitehouse. At the gates they were ushered straight through, they had been expected. Maria was then escorted by four guards to the Oval Office. James was her personal bodyguard now, but even he knew she was entering the safest place in the world. Remaining in the car hadn't worried him. Maria sat outside the Oval Office with the president's secretary as she watched the clock ticking. She was kept waiting outside for twenty minutes. Then she was escorted in by two of the president's security detail. Victoria Owens was alone when they entered. She gestured over to the seating area for Maria to sit down and then joined her on the opposite couch.

"Maria, so lovely to see you again." Victoria looked up at her security and they left the room.

"Madam President, it is my honour. Thank you for the invite."

"Please, we are alone now. Please call me Victoria. As you are now my biggest campaign funder, you at least get that privilege. As did your father. I have ordered us some tea, I trust that is okay? Earl Grey is your favourite, if I remember, Maria? With a slice of lemon?" Victoria spoke with a soft strong voice. Maria had heard her speak a hundred times.

"Yes, thank you. And thanks for remembering." Maria wasn't surprised that Victoria was on the ball. Everything she had seen and read about her said that she was a remarkable woman. Maria had voted for her and spent time helping on her campaign trail with her father.

"How is your mother, Maria? Carly. I know it has only been three months but is she coping better? It must be hard. It will have been a great loss to her. To you both. Your father was a great man." Victoria spoke as she poured the tea.

"She is, Victoria. A little bit better every day. She has thrown herself into her charity work which is good for her. That, the house and her social circles, they keep her busy."

"That's good to hear. She is a remarkable woman. It is times like this when you really need friends around you." Maria could hear the words friends emphasised as the president spoke. It felt like she was there to become friends. She knew Victoria wanted something from her, she just wasn't sure it was to become friends.

Victoria Owens finished making the tea and sat back on the sofa to take a sip. Maria knew that something was coming. It had to be to do with the Brown Institute for starters. This had taken a lot of Maria's time over the past three months. With Alex's work, she feared it was only a matter of time before they were found out. Maria had spent time uncovering more of the family business every day. There were a lot of projects sitting with the board that would be a concern to a president. That could bring down a president and her nation. Victoria had requested her presence at the Whitehouse. As much as presidents needed to request. The invite just had the date and time and come alone. It wasn't to be refused. There was a silence as they both sipped at their tea. Each waiting for the other to talk first.

"Maria, I have a small confession to make." Maria looked directly at her. Her father had told her at an early age the key to business was little talk and lots of eye contact. Silence was the key to any negotiation or interrogation. Maria wasn't sure which one this was going to be.

"Before the tragic developments with your father, I was looking into some of his business concerns. One in particular had started to concern me?" Maria knew what was coming. Another thing her father had said to her was that if you need to distort the truth in business, ensure it is as close to reality as possible.

"Madam President, I think I know where you are going with this and I can assure you it has been dealt with." There was a silence. They both took another sip of tea as if to hold back from the conversation. Someone was going to have to break first. But neither wanted to start with the words 'we have been developing murderers in laboratories.'

"It has, Maria?" Maria knew as soon as Victoria said that, it was going to have to be her to tell the story.

"I am sorry, Victoria, I presume that you were referring to the Brown Institute in Germany? My father started to have concerns also. I have spent a few weeks going through the details and I can assure you, I am as shocked as you." The president nodded at Maria while she drank her tea. Nothing fazed Victoria Owens. Commander and chief of the most powerful nation in the world has its own inner strength. In minutes she had made Maria tell her there was a Brown Institute, it was a problem and she had started to clean it up.

"Upon the death of my father I started to look into his business affairs. He had already put a foreclosure on the site. There seems to have been some medical trials on the site that he did not approve of. When he uncovered these he immediately looked to close the site down."

"Medical experiments?" Maria knew, at that point Victoria knew more than she was letting on. She could read her face. Not many could. But this was one of Maria's gifts.

"Yes, there had been some development on behaviour medication."

"Medication?" The president sipped her tea again, pulling words from a conversation was a trait of Victoria Owens to keep the other person talking. Maria knew that this line of reasoning was going to be a stretch depending on what the president already knew.

"Yes, Mam, Victoria. Medication. There had been extensive research into behaviour patterns and how they could change with the right medication. They had very little success as they could only temporarily change a behaviour. But their aim, I guess, was to see if they could change a behaviour permanently." The president was still silent and looking at her. She knew the trick to good business also.

"From my understanding, their theory behind this was that they would be able to change someone's behaviour pattern completely. They could cure people that had say, murderous or violent tendencies? Imagine if that was possible? They would be able to cure the millions that we have in prisons around the world. Not only in the USA. Releasing billions of pounds back into the economy." Maria knew as always money spoke at every level.

"That would indeed be an amazing achievement, Maria. And, as you say, with outstanding benefits to us. But you say they had little success?"

"That is true. As I said, they had little success in their experiments. I believe their research had taken a turn in the wrong direction. A few doctors at the facility had been curious as to what else they could achieve. And at what stage you could change behaviour. I assure you, my father knew nothing of this. When this was brought to his attention he closed the facility at the cost of millions of dollars to himself and the other investors." Maria wanted to ensure that anything the president had heard was covered in her answer. She didn't want to mention the words children or babies but by saying various stages, that could cover any question that she would be asked. She was also becoming increasingly aware how little the president had said. She knew she was in the presence of a master politician.

"And what of these behaviours, Maria? You said they were temporary?"

"Yes, Victoria. Temporary. Although some longer than others. This is something we are still trying to work through at the moment. I believe some of the patients have had side effects to the treatment. In order to help with that I have set up a rehabilitation foundation. The Michael Mellor Foundation. This is going to ensure that all those people that need treatment and support through the process will get it."

"How many people are we talking about that you would need to start a foundation?" Maria knew that she was going to ask that question but she still needed to try and cover as much of the truth with lies as possible.

"At this time we are still looking into it. The facility had been going for some time in Europe across Germany and France. I have started the Foundation with a five hundred million pound donation. But I assure you, Victoria, we are dealing with it as our number one priority. We have a sense of responsibility to these people as all of this has happened while they were in our care." The president sat back on the sofa. Maria was very similar to her father. She was silver-tongued and there was a trust in her eyes. The President wanted to like her. Everyone wanted to like Maria when they met her.

"That is an amazing contribution, Maria. And, I might say, a fitting tribute to your brother." There was a way that Victoria had said this. Michael's death had made headline news. There was now some doubt in what actually happened. Dr Smith's fake suicide now had the whole crime scene in question. Maria chose to not continue talking of her brother. She now believed that Alex was responsible for his murder. Although there was also an idea in her head that told her her father may have ordered it. He had.

"It is the least we can do. We are cross-referencing and following up on all the patients that visited the facility over this time to ensure they are well and if not to ensure they get the best care money can buy." Maria took another sip of her tea. She had managed to spin the truth into a believable lie. She just didn't know how much the president already knew.

The president had the hard drive. She had the list of names. Dee had visited the Whitehouse and told her everything that Alex had spoken about. The Brown Institute. Michael and Christopher's involvement as far as she knew at that time. Through it all Alex had been a fan of Maria. Alex

31

had told Dee that Maria was an innocent party in all this and could be trusted. As Maria sat across from the president, the president wasn't as sure that was true. She knew Christopher. She knew if there was possibility for a financial reward or power he would have used this technology. The fact that Dee had said it was all for money hadn't shocked the president. The fact that Maria hadn't mentioned a benefit to her father, that did worry her.

After Dee left the Whitehouse Victoria had made her swear to secrecy. Dee agreed, she had played her part and fulfilled Alex's wishes. The president took one look at it, and then the hard drive remained in the presidents drawer. She had been waiting for this moment to hear it from the horse's mouth. Mainly as she didn't know where to start. There was still a doubt in her head on how far this went in the Whitehouse. Since her first day in office Christopher Mellor's name had followed her down the halls. Everyone knew him and everyone had respected him. She had felt over the last few months that allegiance was changing to his daughter Maria. Her name had become more prominent in her house. In Victoria's mind that didn't make her an innocent party.

"Maria, do you know a detective called Alex Keaton?" This took Maria by surprise. The president just coming straight out with Alex's name. How did the president of the United States know Alex? This, for the first time, had her spooked. Maria wasn't so confident in the story she had just spun. If Alex had been in contact with the president, then there was a chance that both Alex and Victoria knew everything. The president certainly knew more that she had thought. Maria was going to have to be careful how she responded now.

"I do. I believe she had been helping my father. With this very issue." There was a pause as she lifted the tea to her mouth. It was cold by now but Maria wanted the president to speak.

"Had?" Another pause. Maria knew she was politely being interrogated.

"Yes, Madam President. I don't believe she is still working for him. Since he died. I have had no contact with her. I have even checked with my staff and nobody seems to have seen her since my father's death."

They were both stone cold with their expressions. They both had secrets neither of them wanted to share. There was a longer silence. The president placed her tea on the tray in front of them and leaned forward towards Maria. She paused again. Maria was holding her breath for a word.

"So talk to me about this Foundation, Maria. Is there anything I can do to help support it?" The interrogation had ended. The president wasn't ready to go after Maria. Not until she had more proof. The conversation continued for another ten minutes and then the president's security entered with almost pinpoint timing of twenty-five minutes.

"Madam President, the Vice President Damion Charles is here to see you."

"Thank you, Andrew. I am sorry, Maria, we will have to call our meeting short. But I am sure we will be meeting again. Real soon." The president stood and shook Maria by the hand.

"Thank you for your time, Madam President." The president had agreed to host a fundraiser at the Whitehouse for the Michael Mellor Foundation. Mainly to stick closer to Maria while she decided her next steps. Maria headed towards the door to leave. Damion Charles entered the Oval Office. Damion had been a decorated hero in Iraq. He was the youngest vice president in history. Victoria chose him as she had no military background herself and she knew that would be good for voters. Damion and Maria exchanged a look as Maria was ushered out of the Oval and down the hallway. Damion Charles spent the next twenty minutes with the president discussing an issue they were having with the Russian president. He had been pushing all of their buttons lately. The president was listening but at the same time she had the conversation with Maria running through her head. She knew there was more to this. Unfortunately she didn't know who she could trust to help her in the Whitehouse.

As soon as Damion left, the president called her head of security back into the Oval Office. Her first words were exactly the same as Maria's when she got back to the car with James.

"We need to find Alex Keaton."

Chapter 2

Alex and Oliver sat watching the comings and goings of the apartment block from the car, awaiting the right person. He wasn't hard to miss, they both tagged him as he walked towards the premises. He was out again in less than five minutes and headed straight down the alleyway. Without saying a word, they were both out of the car. Minutes later they were in the alleyway with him. He hadn't walked more than fifty yards before stopping to take his fix. Still tying off his arm as they approached him behind the dumpster. Oliver grabbed at the syringe in his hand and took it off him.

"Hey, man, what the fuck? That's mine." Alex had her gun out straight in front of her. Oliver was suddenly aware of this. If he had thought about it, he should have been the person to threaten him. Alex was already close to the edge. It was just a natural order that he played the good guy.

"You can have this back. We just need to ask you a few questions." Oliver was already trying to put him at ease. He wanted this to go smoothly. Without any unfortunate events.

"We want to know everything about where you have just been to get that from. Victor Heller's apartment block? Names, layout, the number of people that are in there?" Alex's voice showed the guy she meant business. There was an urgency in the way she spoke. Alex wanted to be in there and resolving the issue. She needed a cure for her issues.

"Are you guys cops?" Oliver turned to say no. Before he could Alex was flashing her badge. She still carried this, she didn't know why, she clearly wasn't a cop anymore. Not in the way she used to be. The work she was doing was putting away bad guys but not legally. Not how her father had taught her.

"Yes, and possession of a class A drug. Is a five to ten-year sentence. Answer our questions and we will look the other way. Don't and..." Alex didn't finish that sentence. Something had stopped her from speaking. Oliver knew it was the thought of what would happen to the guy if he didn't co-operate. Luckily the look in Alex's eyes had shown the guy what not co-operating was going to mean.

"I will tell you anything that you want to know. Just don't throw that shit away. That's all I have." This was a relief to Oliver. He knew that this guy could have easily ended up behind the dumpster permanently if he hadn't met Alex's request. Now he just needed to get them all out of the alley. Alex was in need of a fix. He knew she wouldn't do it in public. She still had some self-control. This guy would be safer in public.

"Okay, we are not going to be able to do this here. We need the layout and everything that you know. I am going to keep this until I am happy you have told us the truth. She will have that gun in her coat at all times. I suggest we walk over to that diner and grab a cup of coffee." The guy got up and walked in front of them. They crossed the road into the diner.

Alex went straight to the booth by the window. They always sat at the window. One eye was always on the street for unwanted visitors. Oliver and the druggie followed her and sat down.

"So draw us a map of the inside of the building. I want you to record everything that you know. And I mean everything." Oliver handed him a napkin and a pen.

"Can I order something?" He wasn't looking at Oliver. He already had been working his way through the menu.

"What?"

"Can I order something? It is a diner? A place where people come to eat?"

"Sure, order whatever you want." Oliver looked at the guy again. At first he had just seen another junkie. On reflection he was sure the guy hadn't eaten for a while. He was thin and unwashed, he looked like he had been living on the streets. Food was something he clearly took whenever he could.

"And you are going to be paying? You know, because I am helping you out and all that?" The druggie still didn't look him directly in the eye. He had been living on the streets and they never looked people in the eye, more head down and hands out.

"Sure we are paying. Order and draw the map. In as much detail as you can. Include the location of any guards or Victor's people. Where they would normally be. Rooms, stairs anything that you can remember."

Alex hadn't spoken. She was still looking at the apartment block. They could only see the corner but Alex felt it drawing her in. The waitress came over and took their order. It was just coffee for Alex and Oliver. The guy had ordered the works. He ate and drew at the same time, drawing as slowly as possible to ensure he got to finish his meal. He explained to them that there were several apartments on the bottom floor. But that wasn't where Victor was. They were all there for either drugs or women. Victor had three men on the bottom floor dealing with the drug dispensary and a further two operating the front door. Five in total. That had Alex interested. He had only been upstairs once. But it was pretty much the same layout. A couple of rooms reserved for higher quality hookers and then Victor's work apartment was at the end of the corridor. Number thirteen. Apparently his favourite number, Victor even had a tattoo of it on his right arm. There were at least another five people on this floor the time that he had been there. Victor liked to surround himself with people. It made him seem bigger than he was. They were going to have to deal with Victor and at least ten more people. Oliver knew the number wasn't going to frighten Alex away from the case. He knew over the last month that the more people that she dealt with, the easier she slept. He wanted her to have some peace.

He did know that Victor didn't stay there at night though. He had tried to score once, around midnight. He got through the front door and before he could get his drugs, there had been a bit of trouble with one of the customers and a hooker. There were only two of Victor's men there. For a moment the man had got the better of them. But only for a moment. He was taken out the back and was never seen again in the apartment block. The body was found floating in Fisherman's Wharf the next day. Oliver handed over a fifty dollar note and the syringe. He told him to get his drugs elsewhere for the next couple of days. If he did return? then he would be locked up as he was under twenty-four hours surveillance now. Oliver was worried he would warn Victor Heller's people for the price of a fix. Alex still wasn't listening.

Oliver knew that the information was going to help. Very few people stayed in the block. It meant people would be easier to count in and out. It also meant they would have another night of bad dreams. The plan would be to rise early and watch the events of the apartment block all day. Picking the right time to make their interest known to Victor.

* * * *

"Thanks for coming, Steve." Fred Keaton opened the door and ushered Steve Marshall into the kitchen where his wife was preparing dinner.

"No problem, Fred, been a while since we have had dinner. A non-formal dinner anyway… Angela, you are looking lovely as ever. I still don't understand how he landed you but I can't disapprove of his taste." Steve handed over the flowers and wine to Angela. Giving her a hug and a kiss on the cheek as he did.

"I tell him how lucky he is every day, Steve. Although I am not sure he believes me." Angela smiled at her husband as she spoke. After thirty-six years of marriage she knew how lucky she had been also.

"Come on, Steve, let's have a beer. Jason is out on the porch and he has some cold ones ready for us." Fred led Steve through the kitchen and out the back door to where his son was waiting. Jason bent down and pulled a beer from the cooler. He handed it over after unscrewing the top.

"Hi, Jason, thanks for that, just what the doctor ordered."

"No problem, Captain." Even though they weren't at work Jason knew the respect you gave a captain. As his father was one also. It was okay that they were on a first-name basis, Fred and Steve. Not Jason. Not yet. They knew why they were all there. It had been three months since Alex's last visit. After six weeks with no contact, they all had begun desperately trying to find her with no success. There was a silence. They were waiting to see who was going to start the conversation. Fred wanted to find his daughter. He didn't want to waste any more time.

"I know I keep asking, Steve, but have you heard anything?" It had been all of three days since he asked Steve that question.

"Nothing, Fred. I have exhausted my contacts. You know that and I know you have too. This special team you talked of that Alex was involved with? Nobody knows anything about it. Especially nothing involving the president or the Whitehouse. I am not sure how high up it goes. But it is clearly too high for me. As nobody is talking." Steve knew the reason for the dinner but came anyway. He knew that they were all becoming desperate. As Alex's captain he knew it didn't reflect well on him either, and he genuinely cared for her. He wanted to do everything he could to get her home.

"Alex wouldn't lie about that? She was going to the Whitehouse. What about the Secretary of State?" Jason believed in his sister. She always told the truth and was straight with all of them. Until this case. Jason and his father knew that she was holding things back from them. They trusted her enough to know that at some point she would tell them everything.

"I know she wouldn't lie. But whatever it was all about? Nobody is talking. I have sent word to the Secretary himself. His office just replied that he didn't know who that was. A two-line reply; that was it. Besides, the Secretary of State's son is dead. Along with Christopher Mellor, one of the most influential people in politics. We can hardly suggest that we believe Alex was working with them both. They are yet to find their murderer. I am sure something is going on behind the scenes but they are not talking to her captain about it. It is clearly above my, our pay grade."

"And nothing turned up from Chris Masters' or James Winters' apartments? Desk? Lockers?"

"No, Fred, as I said. Nothing in any of those places. I have no idea what happened or why to either of my guys? We have CCTV from the marketplace. Alex didn't shoot Chris. I think those rumours came out of panic at the situation. Or someone very cleverly started them to discredit Alex. The shot was from distance. A lot of distance, it was a professional hit, Fred. I don't have a guy on the force that could have made that shot. Someone wanted Chris dead. As for James, he was on his way back into the office to see me when he was shot from three feet away in his car. I told you, before he died, he rang me and said he had something to tell me, but it had to be in person following Chris's death. He was nervous or scared, it was hard to tell it was such a quick call. I have no idea what he wanted to say? They both must have been involved somewhere along the line in this whole thing with Alex and her special squad. They were all involved and all from my precinct, and I knew

41

nothing about it whatsoever. What kind of captain does that make me?" Steve Marshall had been going over this in his mind for the last three months. Alex had disappeared. As far as he was concerned, James and Chris were part of the force looking for her. It looked now that they were involved in the same issues as Alex. The fact they had both been killed in cold blood on the same day that Alex was in town, told him they knew more about what was going on than he did.

Christopher Mellor had ordered the hit on both of them. Christopher's exact orders were to take care of anyone that knew about the files, or anyone who found out about the Institute. Oliver knew how many copies Alex had made at the computer store. That's how he knew one was missing. Chris Masters handed Alex a disc in the marketplace. He didn't know that was the copy Dee had given him. That cost Chris his life. Oliver did this personally. Something he was keeping secret from Alex.

After the marketplace Oliver went straight to James Winters apartment. Knowing he was still working the late shift after Alex and Oliver's visit to the Curle Farm he intended to meet with him in his apartment. James had already heard of the shooting and headed straight to the station. He knew that Chris had the hard drive. It would be the only reason that he would be killed. When Oliver arrived, James was getting into his car already. Oliver followed until they reached a traffic light and pulled alongside. Three bullets ended James Winters connection to the hard drive, Chris and Alex. They all stood drinking their beers in silence again. So much was happening with so little information. They knew Alex was knee-deep in this and the only way to help her, was to get her home first.

What they didn't know was where to start. Jason broke the silence.

"I just think? I think we are going about this all wrong?" Both Fred and Steve looked directly at Jason as he bent back down and pulled them each another beer from the cooler.

"I just think we are thinking about this from the police point of view... Hard not to, I know, given who we are. But the Secretary of State? Presidents, the Whitehouse. That is where Alex ended up. We don't know how she ended up there? We have just accepted that she has. We need to go back to the beginning."

"I think we are going to find that hard to do, Jason. Christopher and Michael Mellor are both dead. Both now it would seem killed, and forgive me for saying this, at a time when we know Alex was close to them. We have lost both her partners on the case in Chris and James which we can only presume is because they knew something, somebody didn't want us to know?" They all knew this to be true. Although they had never admitted it to each other. They knew that Alex's hands were not clean in the whole event. Death was following Alex wherever she went.

"I know but we need to go back even further than the Mellors. That's not where it started. It started with that Jack Quaid case. The suicide, the video she said that she watched. Everything unravelled from that point. He knew something. And whatever it was, Alex followed it to where she is today. I am sure of it. Alex went to Germany because of that tape. Got involved with the Mellors because of that tape. And look where it has led her?" There was a brief silence again. While they each thought back to everything Alex had told them about the Quaid case. It was her first real case since returning back to work. They each remembered she was very vocal about it. About the fact that there was more to Jack Quaid.

"I do agree with you on one level, Jason. It certainly was a strange tape. It made little sense. James, Chris, Alex and I watched it together. Jack Quaid basically, after saying goodbye to his family, apologised for a murders he didn't commit. Mr Howard came home and killed his wife and children with a carving knife. Jack believed he was responsible for that. Seemed to talk a lot in riddles, if I remember. Although he is dead now? He took his own life with a twelve bore. Whatever he knew? Is long gone now?"

"I think we need to go back. Retrace their steps. All their steps. Jack's, Alex's, James', Chris', Michael's, even Christopher Mellor's, if we can? There is a link there. They were all up to something. This special team? I just have a feeling it has them all tied up in it. It has something to do with these murderers as well. I know it. Cleaning up the streets of bad guys has Alex written all over it." They all silently agreed with that. Nobody wanted to mention that Alex was operating outside of the law. Especially in front of Fred. But they all knew that she was capable of anything.

"Dad, you said the same thing. Remember? The Craig Curle case? There is no way that it was a coincidence that Alex was in town. Or that James Winters had a tip to one of the major crimes of the decade? Alex was in there somewhere, I know it. I can feel it. She gave him that credit."

A detective's intuition was a strong thing. Fred knew that his son was turning into a great detective and would make a great captain one day. What he said had made sense. Besides, the current way they were going about it, was getting them nowhere. They needed to step their game up to find Alex.

"I agree with Jason. Let's start on that tomorrow. The three of us. Let's start by reviewing the tape and speak to anyone that knew Jack Quaid. We will follow as much as we can from that point to where we are today. We need to find Alex. I don't know why, and don't tell your mother, but I am getting the increasing feeling that we are running out of time." The door to the kitchen opened and Angela joined them on the porch. They all turned and stopped talking. They didn't want to worry Angela more that she already was.

"Ok, enough talk you three, come in and have some dinner. I am sure you will be back out here afterwards. No shop at the table though. You all know the rules." They all did, even Steve. He had been warned a few times at the table over the years. As Angela re-opened the door they could smell the roast beef.

"I swear, Fred. I don't know how you bagged that woman. I am going to send Cassandra around for cooking lessons." They all followed Angela back into the house.

* * * *

"I swear, Maria, you are turning into you father with all this work. I thought, well, I just thought once we lost him we would start to have dinner at a decent time." Carly was at the table waiting for Maria as she walked into the front door.

"Sorry, Mum. I got sidetracked. I had the board meeting and then the Whitehouse and then I needed to go back to the office." Maria walked over to the table and kissed her mother.

"I will try harder, I promise." Maria took off her coat and handed it to James. He disappeared with it and left them alone at the dinner table.

"So how was the meeting with the president? It must have been exciting? One on one? Not many people get to do that, Maria. Other than you and your father, that is." Maria sat next to her mother. The table was still set for four people. Her mother still hadn't stopped this. One of the staff had done it by accident. At first it upset Carly but ever since she had asked for it to remain that way. Maria ignored it. It was something for her mother to deal with on her own, eventually.

"It was really good. I did feel strange sitting in the Oval Office. You see it on TV but actually being there. She is a very astute lady. Dad really knows how to back a winner. We spoke a little, she sends her best to you and she has agreed to help us with the Michael Mellor Foundation."

"Is that what it was about? The Foundation? Did you tell her everything that your father had found out? I still cannot believe what those doctors were trying to do to those poor children." Maria didn't answer the question with the truth. Keeping her mother from the truth was something she was keen to do. Her father kept it from her so Maria knew that was her job now. The Foundation had only been set up as a distraction to the real stories behind the Institutes. Having her mother help run the Foundation meant that she would still be a part of it. As her father had said, a lie needed to be very close to the truth. They had told Carly there had been some rogue doctors testing synthetic DNA. It had worked and she was totally behind helping them clear things up. The added benefit was that nobody ran a charity like her mother. She could move mountains when she wanted to.

"I think so, and it just felt like she missed Dad. They were close friends. I am sure she will want to keep close for any re-election campaigns also." All presidents needed money for campaigns. Victoria Owens had been lucky enough to secure the Mellors. Or so she thought. Now she was wondering whether she chose them or she was in fact chosen to be their president.

"I am sure they were, he practically put her in the seat. Not to mention the time we all spent on the campaign. Not that it wasn't the right choice. I think she is making a fine president. She will help keep our country safe."

The food arrived at the table and water was poured for them. They didn't acknowledge the fact. These things happened like clockwork in the Mellor household.

"Did you get to see any more of the Whitehouse? Or more importantly, the vice president?" Maria could sense the tone in her mother's voice. It was playful, she liked that. It was good to see her mother in high spirits.

"The Whitehouse, no. I was in and out. But I did manage a polite wave at the vice president." Maria was now looking directly at her mother. She was waiting for the next sentence as if she didn't know what was coming. It was going to be something to do with how young or handsome or single he was.

"Youngest in history, wasn't he?" Carly threw the comment out as she started on her dinner.

"Yes, I think I read that somewhere." There was a smile on both their faces as they spoke.

"If I recall, he is single as well?" They both knew this already. Carly didn't need to mention it again. She had quite often spoke of Damion over the whole campaign.

"Yes, I read that too, Mum. Six foot one as well, a Scorpio, I believe."

"Just saying, dear, just saying. Quite handsome, so they say." There was a giggle from both of them. The rest of the evening continued along the same line of conversation. Maria being single and there being a multitude of suitors out there for her. Her mum had been quite intuitive with her first guess though. Maria's heart had missed a beat when Damion Charles entered the Oval Office earlier that day. It hadn't been the first time that they had met. Just the first time without Michael on her arm.

* * * *

Oliver sat with his back against the headboard as Alex slept across his lap. The sweats were there and he kept a cold damp cloth on the side of the bed to try and cool her down. He knew Michael Mellor was in there somewhere with her. His name would come out of her lips nightly now. She had somehow crossed him with her own demons. Alex reached out in her dream and Oliver pulled her hand back down. With that she awoke. She didn't say anything, she just looked up at Oliver. He grabbed the cloth and wiped her brow.

"Is it morning?" Oliver just nodded in return. There was a faint smile across Alex's face. She knew that she would get her fix today. That would give her the peace she needed. A few nightmare-free nights. Alex laid there for another ten minutes before moving. Her head started to fill with the events to come. That was settling to her. When she finally arose she went and showered alone. Oliver knew to leave her alone; it was her time. Her time to prepare for the events of the day.

It seemed to Oliver it was long time ago when he didn't join her on her quest. When he would only play a small part. Making sure cameras were down or security alarms were off. Now he was a full-time partner. He didn't want to leave Alex alone. For her own protection as much as his feelings to keep her safe. After showering they both headed back out to Fisherman's Wharf. They didn't expect the drug trade to be in full flow before lunchtime. When they arrived outside of Victor's apartment block, it was deserted. They had to wait for an hour for the first people to arrive. Two and a half before Victor himself made an appearance. Most of the time had been spent in silence. As soon as Victor arrived though the conversation started to flow. The napkin drawing that they had obtained from the drug user showed them the entrance and the suspected positions of Victor's men. Oliver's plan was to take out the ground floor himself. Leaving Alex to take the first floor and Victor. Over the last few months Oliver had started to realise this was no longer just about the Brown Institute individuals. It had become more primal than that with Alex. This had turned into good versus evil in her mind. With Alex playing the part of good. If you were affiliated with a Brown Institute child, then you were as guilty as they were. Oliver's mind wandered back often the Grayling case. He had been watching Alex from afar that evening. Paul Grayling was following the van that carried the dead girl. When the two men exited the van and prepared to move the body, Alex dispatched them as quickly as she could. Not a second thought. She hadn't known their role in the murder or murders, just that they had been willing to transport a body was enough now for Alex to kill them. They had chosen to work for Paul Grayling and there were a dozen people out there that had died because of him. If you associated yourself with a Brown Institute baby, that was enough for Alex now. Oliver knew she was no longer playing by the rules she had set herself in the beginning. This didn't worry him. He believed in her. Besides, he was now associated with a Brown Institute victim. The work they were doing though was for the right reasons. They reminded each other of that often.

Alex and Oliver continued to count the people in and out of the building most of the lunchtime, and late into the afternoon. As much as twenty-four at any one time were inside. As the night drew in the people started to leave. Without mentioning it, they were both getting worried that Victor could leave at any moment. Alex broke the silence in the car.

"I reckon we are down to eight, plus whoever was in there last night?"

Oliver nodded. It was time. They both got out of the car and crossed the street to the apartment block.

* * * *

"I have read all of Alex and James Winters' notes on the case. Even Chris Masters' report. There doesn't seem to be anything that we didn't know written down. I am considering reading Jack Quaid's journal. Maybe Alex found something in there that everyone else will have missed? We know how good she is?" Jason always considered his sister to be a better detective than him. So did his father although he never actually said it. Alex had the confidence to join a different station house for that reason. She didn't want to be just the captain's daughter.

"I have watched the tape at least a dozen times and I am not sure what Alex saw in this that I didn't. I think the tape just distracts from the whole thing." Jason sat opposite his father at the kitchen table. They weren't breaking the rules of the house as his mother had left for the evening for dinner with a friend.

"I looked over a few of those books. They were the ramblings of a mad man, I think, Jason. Dinosaurs and moon landings, that type of thing. I wouldn't put too much effort into them. There must be something else. Something not in the report, something Alex has kept to herself? Problem is, if your sister doesn't want you know something, wants to keep it hidden? You will not find it out."

"I know, Dad. We will not and Alex didn't tell anyone what she was thinking. Alex was on her own with this. There is no reference to anything out of the ordinary." Jason shrugged his shoulders.

"What about the Michael Mellor report? The incident in the nightclub when Alex caught the guy red-handed stabbing that young lad? The one Alex changed in favour of the Mellors?"

"To me? It looked like he was guilty. At least that is what the first draft had said. Captain Marshall confirmed that was her statement. But by changing the report? Well, that is what got her to Germany. She was onto something? Captain

Marshall believed in her. On her return she told them that it all had come to nothing. I know her, Dad. If that was the case, she wouldn't have gone to Italy. That's not Alex, is it? None of that is true. I think she found something in Germany and then it made her go to Italy. I think for whatever reason? She went there for Michael." Alex wasn't the type to go off on a wild goose chase. She was a very good detective, always followed the evidence. This trip to Italy bothered both of them. They knew what Alex had said, they knew she had been keeping the real information back from them.

"And the wife? Jack Quaid's wife. She met with her a couple of times. James and Chris met with her also. Do you think she knows anything that will be of use to us?"

"I think that is an in person conversation, Dad. I have put a call in to her. She will be home around seven thirty. I was going to go around before heading home?" Dee had not been surprised at the call. She had expected that even though the president had sworn her to secrecy someone was going to want to speak to her.

"Okay, I think that is a good idea. If anyone knows about Jack Quaid, it must be her." Fred got up and turned the kettle on.

"I would say so too, Dad. But apparently they had been broken up for some time. I am hoping whatever this is? May have been the reason. It will give us a place to start." Both Fred and Jason were increasingly having the same worrying thought but too scared to say it.

"She is going to be okay, isn't she, Dad? I can't help think that she is in trouble." Jason would have never said this if his mother had been home. But his dad was his captain too. He knew he would take it in the right context.

"I really don't know, Jason. The longer this goes on, the more worried I am about it. I have been following cases across the country. There have been sightings of a woman and a man. The Real Avengers or whatever the press is calling them. But they are over so quickly and not seen again. She is not alone wherever she is. She is always seen with a guy. So that is some comfort."

"I think that is her, Dad. I suppose that is one thing, that she is not alone. Do you think it is the same guy that pulled up outside here and dropped her off?"

It was Fred's turn to shrug his shoulders. It was a relief to both of them that she wasn't alone. They had watched as murderer after murderer had been taken care of. Some known. Some not so known. Not until the police had dug deeper. The police force was buzzed with the news. Divided in camps of support for them and real dislike for the justice that was being dished out. Jason and his father were on opposite camps with Jason being supportive of the work. He didn't mention it in front of his father though or other senior members of the force. Something he reserved for his friends and wife. He respected his father too much to embarrass him. Above all, his father was his captain.

* * * *

Oliver was trying to keep up with Alex as she crossed the road. He managed to reach her before she got to the front door, pulling on her shoulder to stop her in her tracks.

"Alex, we need to go in slowly. This isn't the time for all guns blazing" Alex was only half listening to him but he had managed to give them a moment so they could compose themselves.

"Nice and slow, Alex, just follow my lead." Oliver went first to the door. He pressed the buzzer on the wall on the right-hand side of the door. A voice came over the intercom.

"Yes?"

"I am a friend of Victor." The buzzer sounded and released the door. They didn't know if that was going to work. Something Oliver had thought about after the druggie had left the diner. Was there a code word to get in? should have been one of the first questions. He figured that nobody other than druggies would have known it was run by Victor Heller. Oliver pulled at the door and walked in. Slowly followed by Alex. The guy from the alley had told them to go to the second apartment. They followed his instructions as if they had been there a million times. Passing the two armed guards that were standing protecting the door. There was no real security to speak of. Just two guys on the door. These were just hired goons that worked for Victor. Hard men but not in Oliver's league. It didn't take a lot to take down a druggie or someone looking for a good time with a prostitute. Heading to the apartment was a plan to buy them time to look around and ensure they knew the layout of the building. Alex had wanted to go in fast and take them by surprise. Oliver convinced her it was better to take their time. They didn't want any alarms or more unwanted guests at the apartment block. The map they had been drawn was pretty accurate, the druggie had certainly earned his dinner. The first apartment door was open. There was a girl in plain sight inside. Dressed in stockings and suspenders. Several other apartments were open. They presumed girls were in them too. The second apartment door was closed. No drugs were to be on show. That was part of Victor's rules. Oliver knocked at the door and it was opened by another of Victor's men. Three more were inside. Alex followed him in and the door was closed behind them.

Victor's family were wealthy. They had made hundreds of millions by investing in the property market. There was no need for him to be doing this. As soon as they walked into the room, they knew it was an ego trip for Victor. There were piles of drugs everywhere. Everything from hash to cocaine and it was stored as if in a warehouse. Victor had grown up rebelling against his family and watching too many bad gangster movies. That mixed with what the Institute had done to him meant that there was only ever really going to be one outcome.

"So, mate. How can we help you? Blow, weed, what is your pleasure?"

Oliver just looked at him. He didn't say a word.

"I guess by the look of his missus, it's her that needs a fix. Proper cold sweats you have going on there, love." Oliver turned to Alex. At the same time, they both pulled out their guns and shot the four guys without making a sound. Silencers on the guns had kept the whole thing under wraps. Oliver was a crack shot. Both of his guys had been taken down in head shots. Two bullets. Alex wasn't as talented. The first had gone down fast but the second took three shots. None of the victims made a sound as they hit the floor. Alex could feel the rush as she pulled the trigger. It was a huge release. It was addictive though. As they hit the floor Alex was looking for the next person to take care of.

"So what now?" Oliver knew what now. It was a prompt for Alex. He knew they needed to get on with it. She needed to get on with it. It was her issue to resolve. He was only there for support.

"We take the two guys outside. But we need to keep the girls quiet. They will see it. We can't risk them shouting upstairs." Alex was in full workflow mood. Planning her next steps and ensuring she got what she wanted. What she wanted was to take care of Victor Heller.

"Give me your badge. They won't argue with a badge. You take them out and then I will deal with the girls. They will not hear the shots and the first thing they will see when they come out is me. Armed police." Alex handed over her badge to Oliver. They turned and opened the door to the hallway. Walking out the two guys were still standing by the door. They clearly hadn't heard anything. Alex took the lead and took them both out with a single shot each. Her full focus had returned. Behind Alex Oliver had his gun raised in case she had missed. She didn't. Alex was clear to take the stairs. As the guards hit the ground Oliver could hear the girls moving. He stood by the front door with his badge and gun straight in front of him. The first girl that they had seen made an appearance at the door. Took one look at him and turned and closed the door. Police weren't something they wanted to deal with. Oliver had made a good call.

Alex started to climb the stairs.

* * * *

56

"Finding them has to be our top priority, James. We have too much tied up in the Institutes. All of them. Alex Keaton knows everything, I am sure of it. My father, my father is, was a show boater. He was the ultimate villain. Just before he deals with you, he will tell you his plan for world domination." Maria was sat at her father's desk in his office. This had now become hers. James was surprised at how she spoke of her father. She had always seemed to have no interest in the comings and goings of the Mellor house. Maria was always in the background but had paid attention to everything. The years cleaning up after Michael had made her very aware of her surroundings, and what her father was capable of.

"I understand, Maria." Maria was silent.

"Oliver is very resourceful and he chose her over my father. After years of service." James remained silent. It was clear Maria was playing things over in her head.

"He could have tortured everything out of my father. He could do that, couldn't he? That's the kind of thing he could do?" She was looking at James now. He just nodded. James knew what Oliver was capable of, he had seen it first-hand. Christopher Mellor had employed skilled negotiators with a wide skill set.

"Everything could collapse James… Everything! I know that if Alex wanted answers she would have got them."

"I understand, Maria."

"Do you, James? Do you understand? Sometimes I wonder. I can't believe that in this day and age we can't find two people roaming the country killing people? It's not like they are hiding all the time. This is ridiculous." Maria was getting herself wound up about this now.

"I have another meeting tomorrow. With the research department. I think they have the breakthrough we have been waiting for to help clear this mess up. And yet Alex and Oliver are still running loose. They could fuck all this up." Maria threw a pen onto the desk in front of her. James had never seen her this angry. James stood still and didn't say a word. He was waiting for Maria to calm down. Maria sat staring out the window for a few minutes before turning to James.

"I know you are doing all you can, James. Sorry for shouting. Let's just see if we can do more. I will feel a lot safer in everything once this is cleared up." The tone in her voice had changed. It was back to being soft. James wasn't sure which was scarier.

"I will get straight on it, Mad… Maria." James turned out of the office and headed towards the kitchen. Stopping en route to take his phone out and send just one text. It simply said "She will take this search off me. You need a plan."

Oliver could feel the text as it vibrated in his pocket.

Chapter 3

"Hi, Mrs Quaid, we spoke on the phone." Jason stood on the porch as Dee opened the door to him.

"Hi, yes, come in, come in. And it's not Mrs Quaid anymore. I don't think, I don't think I can use that now my husband is dead and we were already separated? Or I should only be using that. It is all too confusing. Dee will be just fine." Jason followed her into the house. Dee headed over to the fridge.

"Can I get you a drink? Tea, coffee? Or a cold one. I am going to have a cold one, beer, I mean. Would you like one? Or are you still on duty? Sorry, didn't think." Dee reached into the fridge and pulled herself out a beer.

"No, I am not on duty, ma'am. So a beer would be good."

"Okay, but not ma'am either, makes me sound like the Queen. Dee, just Dee."

"Okay, just Dee." Dee took another beer from the fridge and headed over to the sofa, gesturing to Jason to sit down.

"So what can I do for you, Detective? You said on the phone you had a few questions regarding my husband's case? I must say, I was surprised to hear that after such a long time.

I thought the whole thing had been closed." Jason had. He had also deliberately not told her his last name. He didn't want her to know that he was Alex's brother. He wanted to hear what she had to say cold and without any distractions.

"Yes, that's right, Dee. I was just reviewing old case files of one of our detectives and I noticed that this was the last case she worked on." Dee knew that he meant Alex. Alex had explained everything to her when she returned from Grayling. How she hadn't been at work since returning from Italy. How she ended up mixed up with the Mellor family and the quest that she found herself on. As with the president, Alex had sworn Dee to secrecy. Dee felt partly responsible for all of this. Like she had to protect her, given it was her ex-husband that had started Alex down this path.

"Oh, that was ages ago now? That can't have been the last case?" Dee played her part well. She purposely didn't say her last case. She would try her hardest to keep the secrets she had.

"Yes, I know, but the detective running the case has been…" Jason paused. He didn't know what to say next, has been missing? Has been a vigilante on the run ever since? Is probably now murdering murderers for a living? The pause was a few seconds too long. Dee felt like she had to fill the void.

"Has been what, Detective?" Dee was also keen to know what he already knew. It would make it easier for her to keep her cover.

"Has been missing. The detective has been missing and we are just following her last footsteps to see if we can ascertain where she is, or whether or not this case has anything to do with her disappearance."

Dee took a swig of beer. She didn't need to pause to think, she had a drink to disguise this. Over the last few months she had ran the stories over in her head that she would tell, should she be questioned.

"That is such a shame. I presume you mean the woman then. Alex, wasn't it? I was visited by a few of your colleagues, Detective. She seemed a very nice woman from what I remember. And you are here tonight because you think I would know something, do you, Detective? That would help you find her? Somehow this may be tied back to my husband's case?"

"Jason. Call me Jason. I don't know, to be honest. We are just looking at it from all angles. Can you tell me anything? As far as the notes read it was a straightforward case? Nothing really stands out as to why she would leave her job? Or indeed not contact her family or friends?" Jason leaned in, as if to listen intently to the answer. Part of his police training had taught him the importance of body language. Especially when interviewing. He knew it would put more pressure onto Dee. It didn't faze her as much as he had hoped. Dee had been expecting visitors long before now. She knew that this wasn't over. There was just too much interest in the story that Alex had told for it to stop. Other people were always going to follow.

"Straightforward is a strange word for my husband's suicide." Jason felt guilt as soon as those words came out of her mouth. He realised he was thinking like a detective. He should have been more compassionate around the death of her husband. He was about to apologise when Dee continued.

"But, yes, I would guess it's as good a word as any. I don't really know what to say to you, Jack was a troubled man." He was thankful that she glossed over it so he didn't go back to the point.

"I understand that you were estranged? How long before, well, before the tragic events of that evening?" He knew that was better. At least he acknowledged it.

"Yes, I suppose we were. Estranged is an odd word, don't you think? I moved out about six months previous. I suppose, I always thought deep down that we would be together again. Clearly that wasn't going to be the case. Jack had theories and thoughts, you see. That weren't the same as everyone else. The more I think about it, the more I understand why he felt he didn't belong here anymore. He was always quite withdrawn into himself. Saying that, I do miss him, Detective." Dee fell silent. It had been a while since she had thought about Jack in that way. She had been trying to remember him with all the positive points. The flowers, the attention he used to lavish onto her. It was all a little tainted now that she knew of his condition. What she mistook for attention had been obsession. A present he had been given from the Brown Institute.

"I am sorry for your loss, Dee." Jason gave her a moment. She was clearly deep in thought.

"It says from the notes that you met with Detective Keaton a few times over your husband's case?" He was trying to keep eye contact with Dee. He wanted to see the expressions on her face to tell if there was more to discover.

"I suppose I did. I think the first time she came to tell me he had died. Then again at our house, I know I shouldn't have been there. It was only a brief conversation that night. Then at the station when we watched the tape? She was late. She was always late. I presume you have watched the tape also?"

"I have. Do you have any idea why your husband was saying the things he was saying? About the Howard case? There is nothing in Alex Keaton's notes to explain his actions. Although we clearly know now he had nothing to do with the murders. It did seem to me at first that he was confessing to the crime?" Dee looked away from Jason. Jason took this as a sign a lie was coming. It was partly to do with that. Partly due to that tape. She hated the thought that Jack's last thoughts were that he had done something to cause their murders. She knew Jack's emotions were always strong. Part of his condition. She knew it would have been hurting him. She had just wished she had known sooner and they could have faced his condition together.

"As I said, Jack was a complicated man. I think he had just got his wires crossed. I believe it was something to do with a cab ride. Sometimes his mind could wander like that. He would start down a thought path and it would lead him somewhere that made no sense. I presume you have read his journal? That clearly shows how sometimes Jack would lose reality. Well, clearly he had on that day, as he took his own life." It was hard not to agree with that statement. Nothing as powerful as a statement losing the man that you loved. Dee knew that. Although Jason already started to doubt what she was saying. She had started to move in her chair. Like she was uncomfortable. That was another sign of someone that was lying. The comment about him ending his life was meant to close down the conversation, he was sure of that.

"I think the report said that she visited you one more time after the tape? Is that correct? You didn't mention that one?" Dee took another swig from the bottle as she ran the meetings through her head. Ones she knew that they would have on record. The last few times that she had met Alex always ended with same promise to keep this between them until the time was right.

"Yes, I think so? She was always so busy. Yes, I think one more time and then the other two gentlemen came and visited me a few times. They were concerned for the detective also." Dee was keen to ensure that Jason didn't only think Alex was involved. She had already shared some information with the police. She presumed he would know at least that much. But she wasn't going to give up the information unless asked.

"Yes, that would be Doctor Chris Masters and Detective James Winters?"

"Yes, I think that was their names. They didn't say she was missing though. Not that I recall." They had said she was missing. Dee lied to play down the meeting.

"They were worried about her. I think that is what they had said. They only came to see if she had been in touch. She hadn't. Not that I would have expected it, Detective. We only met a few times. She did always seem in a rush to get somewhere though. Always running at a hundred miles per hour. I guess that is what makes a good detective?" Jason knew only too well that was Alex. She would always throw herself into her work. Whatever this was now, had Alex in overdrive.

"And the last time you saw her, Dee. How did that go? What did you talk about?" Dee knew that she hadn't given him anything yet. She had just glossed over the fact that they had met.

"She had just come back from a trip. She just wanted to check up on me. Make sure I was okay. That was all, I think. I understand she had just lost someone close to her. Her partner or someone? Police partner? I guess she knew how it felt. She was a very nice woman. Probably hadn't seen me at my best. It was almost to just reassure me that there was nothing in that tape. It was as you said a straightforward case." Jason wasn't buying what she was saying. Dee looked too uncomfortable for his liking. She was speaking too fast as if to blurt out a lie. So that it didn't taint her mouth.

"That will be when she returned from Italy then?" Jason knew what he had said.

"Yes, I think so? I remember her saying how lovely the churches were. Although she didn't get to St Peter's. I think she wishes she had. Is that going to be all? I really don't have anything else to say. If you like, you could always talk to his father. I am sure he will be glad of the company." Dee knew as soon as those words were out of her mouth it was a mistake. He knew of the letter. She knew that Jack's dad wasn't sworn to secrecy on anything. She was going to have to speak to him before the detective did. Or all of this could unravel quickly.

"Thanks. I had planned on doing that already." Jason was keen to let Dee know this wasn't going away. He would be following up with everyone.

"Good, I hope that was of use, Detective. If you don't mind, I really need to take a shower. You can really tell I have been to the gym this evening." Jason finished his beer in one go and placed the empty bottle on the table. He stood to leave.

"Yes, sorry, Dee, thanks you have been ever so helpful."

"I do hope you find your detective, Detective." Dee was almost ushering him out the door now. Jason said his goodbyes and headed to the car. As soon as he sat in the driver's seat he rang his father.

"Hi." Fred picked up straight away. He had been sitting by the phone, waiting for the call.

"Hi, Dad, it's me."

"Well, how did it go with Mrs Quaid? What did she say about Jack?"

"Everyone seems to think that Jack Quaid was just a little bit crazy. Including his wife. Which would explain the books you have looked over and the confession on the tape. She stuck by her original story that we have written down for timing of separation. Six months. Met with Alex a few times but nothing out of the ordinary." Jason stopped.

"I sense a but coming, Jason?" Fred knew when there was more on Jason's mind. Even over the phone he could tell his tone of voice.

"She is lying to me though, \dad, I know it. There is something that she isn't telling me. She couldn't sit still at points or look me in the eye. She hid some of it well. But I know there is more."

"What do you think she is lying about?"

"About Alex. I didn't want to push it, as I hadn't told her who I was. Just that I was looking into her disappearance. The records show that Alex went back to see her after her visit to the Brown Institute. She has seen Alex after that. She mentioned Italy and the churches. Alex mentioned those to us too, if you remember, over dinner. That was at least a month, maybe two, after the record shows she visited Dee. She knows more than she is telling us?" There was a silence from the other end of the phone.

"So what do you want to do about it?"

"I don't know yet. Let me sleep on it, Dad, and we can have a conversation tomorrow. I don't want to spook her into anything. She maybe our only lead so far. I also want to talk to Jack's dad. She mentioned that I should. But as soon as she did, her face changed. I don't think she meant to say that. I am hoping that he knows something too."

"Okay, come around tomorrow, we can discuss it." Fred hung up the phone. Jason sat thinking about what had just happened. His instincts told him he was getting closer to something. Taking this back to the beginning was starting to pay off.

* * * *

Alex climbed the stairs to the first floor. As she did she realised that the layout was the same as the ground floor. To her right was another open door with a woman sitting in a chair in the distance. She was watching TV but the chair had been positioned so that she could see the comings and goings of the hallway. As she passed the door, the woman got up. She was dressed in black underwear with stockings and suspenders on. She was blonde like the girl downstairs but prettier. She filled every inch of her underwear perfectly. Victor had kept all the quality upstairs, mainly for his own use. Occasionally for special customers.

Alex carried on walking to the door at the bottom of the corridor. Number thirteen. Just as the map had showed them. She knocked on the door. Within seconds it opened. The guy standing in front of Alex was bigger than Craig Curle back at the farm. Craig had taken twenty bullets before he hit the ground. The guy in front of her now took one. Alex shot him squarely between the eyes at point-blank range. Before he had hit the ground, Alex was in the apartment. There were three men and one woman. The woman was sitting with who she recognised as Victor on the sofa, the other two men were standing in the middle of the room. Alex fired five shots. There were screams of pain from both men but they were brief before they had been dealt with. The woman was screaming as Victor jumped forward for his gun that lay on the glass table in front of them. Alex put a bullet through it. The glass shattered and the gun fell out of his reach.

"Don't!" Alex meant business. Victor pulled his hand back from the area of the table. Alex could feel the blood pumping through her veins. This had been the fix that she needed. With each shot, Alex felt calmer. In her head it had happened in slow motion. That's how she could be so focused. In real life it had been a matter of seconds. Victor was on his feet.

"Who the fuck are you to come into my house?" Victor's chest was out and his arms were waving in the air as if he had been a bad gangster on one of the cop shows that Alex had watched as a kid.

"Sit down!" Alex meant what she said. She was purposeful and in charge. She was keen that Victor knew this.

"I said…"

"I said sit the fuck down! Now!" Victor took another look at Alex. She had taken out his whole crew in less than a minute. This wasn't going to be his time to stand tall. He sat back on the sofa and put his arm around the girl that was still sitting there. She had stopped screaming, if only to hear what Alex had to say. The tears were rolling down her face. But she remained silent.

"I have a question to ask you. How many, Victor?" Those words had come to mean so much to Alex. How many, they were her justification. Her justification for what was going to come next.

"How many what? What the fuck are you on?" Victor laid back as if he didn't have a care in the world. He just pulled the girl closer to him. Almost as a shield. Alex had no doubt that is what he would have used her for if he had the chance.

"How many people have you killed, Victor?" Alex was looking directly at him now. He knew she meant business.

"I haven't killed anyone? What are you, police? Go on, fucking arrest me. I will be out in a couple of hours. Do you even know who the fuck you are dealing with?" Alex didn't say a word. The look on Victor's face made Alex just want to shoot him there and then. She couldn't, she needed to know. Somewhere deep inside it gave her a relief to know the number of people who had lost their lives by his hand. The guards. They deserved it. They deserved what they got due to working for the guy. They had a choice and they chose to live this lifestyle. Victor didn't. It didn't mean he deserved to live though.

"You're no fucking police. So what is it you want? Drugs? Money? I have plenty of both. Just take what you want and fuck off. I am busy." Victor pulled the girl closer. She was almost sitting on his lap by now.

"Get out." Alex gestured to the girl and pointed the gun at her. She checked with Victor. He didn't want her to move.

"I said get the fuck out or you will end up like the rest of them!" She checked again with Victor and he released her. She did as she was told. Alex watched her as she left to ensure she didn't jump her from behind.

"I said how many, Victor? How many people have you killed? Had killed in your short pathetic life?" Victor was now moving with less confidence. His shield was gone and he was well aware of his surroundings.

"None. I haven't killed anyone. I just deal drugs, that is all. Maybe the odd girl now and again?" Victor was lying and Alex knew it, they all lied. They all tried to pretend, but Alex knew better.

"That is not all, Victor. You see, I know you. I know all about you. You were born to be a killer. It is in your nature. So I am going to ask you one more time. How fucking many?" Alex spoke with confidence. This was her place. This is who she was now. She was the judge and jury for these people.

"What the fuck are you talking about? I am no killer? Look, I am not sure where you got your information from but it's wrong. My family are rich. I mean, real rich. Let's just forget what has happened here, neither of us saw anything and none of these people will be missed. The girls downstairs will do as they are told. They are whores, they work for me. We can come to some arrangement?" Victor was almost pleading at that point. He knew Alex had no issue killing, there were three dead bodies in the room to prove that. A deal was always going to be offered by Victor. Alex knew the type. First they defend by saying it wasn't them and then they offered money. It was the next level bargaining. People with money always believed that it could solve anything. It was money that had started all this. Money and power. That is what had the Mellors interested, that was how Alex had gotten herself mixed up in the case. Following the money.

Money was never important to her. Alex watched him as he squirmed in front of her. Alex was very calm now. He could tell in the way she spoke to him.

"I want a number, Victor, then we will come to a deal."

Victor leaned back again. He felt that a deal was on the table. He was confident that money could buy his way out of anything. It had for his entire life. Alex's voice had changed from screaming at him to gentle. She was trying to get him onside. If he had known her better, he would have known that wasn't a good thing.

"What number?"

"The number. How many people have you killed, Victor? Or ordered to be killed?" Victor knew what she meant. He knew she wanted the truth. He just didn't know why?

"And then we are done?"

"We are. Other than the little deal we talked about." Alex nodded her head. She knew this was going to work. Victor crossed his legs and stretched his arms out to make himself comfortable.

"Odd request, little lady. I don't know, sixteen, seventeen. I lose count. I do it myself when I can. You have to show you are the boss. It is bad, I know, but a man has to do what he has to do in this game. You can't let them disrespect you and all that. These people need to be taught a lesson. You feel me?" Alex could hear the change in his voice. His confidence was returning. He thought money was saving him. The ghetto accent was coming out of his mouth. He wanted to be a gangster. He loved being a gangster. But that was not who he really was. Alex could not hold her temper anymore.

"You went to Yale? What do you mean, you feel me? You have an English degree? Feel what, for fuck's sake? You don't come from the streets, you do know that, don't you?" Victor's face changed. She knew more about him than he thought. Her voice had stepped up again. He could tell that he had pissed her off.

"You are not a gangster, Victor, you trained as a lawyer." Alex raised her gun. He didn't deserve the attention she was giving him. As she did, a gunshot rang past her ear. She turned to see the girl she had let go walking into the room firing at her. A second and then a third, it was clear the girl had never shot before as the bullets were flying closer to Victor than to Alex. Alex fired one in her shoulder and she dropped the gun. As she did, Victor had charged at Alex and knocked the gun out of her hand.

"Not so fucking big now, are you, bitch? Did you feel that… you feel me now? You feel me now?" Victor grabbed the gun and stood above Alex.

"You come into my house. Disrespect my house. Kill my fam. Who the fuck do you think you are, bitch? This is going to be—"

Two shots fired. One hit Victor's shoulder, the other Victor's leg. Oliver was standing in the doorway. He hadn't shot to kill Victor. That was Alex's job. He was purely lending a hand. Alex grabbed the gun back as Victor fell and she stood up. Victor and the girl were on the floor in pain. Oliver left the room and went back downstairs. That was enough involvement for him.

"I thought we were having a—" Victor didn't get to finish his sentence. Alex put a bullet straight between his eyes. Seventeen was the official number. Victor was never getting to eighteen.

"I hope you felt that," Alex almost whispered the words. She stepped over the body as she left. The girl was still crying in pain on the floor. Alex paid her no attention and headed to the door.

"I will kill you, bitch…" The girl cried out as Alex exited the room. A moment later Alex returned. The girl was never going to make good on her words. Two bullets ended any chance of her killing Alex. Alex headed back down the stairs. When she got to Oliver she took the file out of the bag they had carried in and left it on the stairs. Her fingerprints were all over the file now. She wasn't hiding this anymore. She wrote the number seventeen on the front cover.

* * * *

"Morning, my dear." Carly could hear her approaching. Maria used to tease her for her supersonic hearing.

"Morning, Mum, you know you don't have to make me breakfast, don't you? Sandy will be really upset if you mess up her kitchen again." Carly was beating batter for pancakes as Maria entered the kitchen.

"I know, but I like to give her Saturday mornings off. Besides, I like cooking for you. Make sure you are eating properly. That's a mum's job." Carly had tried to cook breakfast for her whole family once a week. Christopher and Maria had generally ensured they were there. Michael had spent most Saturday mornings nursing a hangover. Carly always sent pancakes to his room but they were very rarely eaten.

"Okay, but I don't need a half a dozen like last weekend. There are only two of us now. I couldn't move till midday." Carly poured orange juice for them both and coffee. Maria didn't mean to point out the obvious so she didn't mention it again. Her mother had still cooked for the four of them. The batter recipe had been the same. She just picked up the paper and sat reading while her mother made stacks of pancakes.

"You are turning into your father, you know that? I watched you straight to the finance page. There was a time you would never pick up the paper. Always magazines. To see what the latest fashion is? And who is wearing what? They were the most important things in my little girl's life." Maria placed the paper down.

"I still do that, Mum. I just try to have other interests too. More grown-up ones." Carly placed the first stack of pancakes onto Maria's plate. Maria gave her the look as if to say how many?

"I am glad to hear it. There is some syrup in the fridge, get it out for me." Maria did as she was told and came back to sit at the counter with her mother.

"So what are your plans for this morning?"

"Do you know what, Mum? I don't know? There is nothing in my diary. Which I thought was odd. I was thinking about going do to the club to see if it was okay. It has been months since I have been there. Maybe to the hairdressers. Feels like months since I have done that too. Did I really just say that? I think you are right, I am turning into my father.

Maybe I should just buy some clippers and have done with it." There was a slight smile on both of their faces. Maria's father, on one of his rants about time, had worked out how long he spent in the barber's chair in a year. When he realised it was over a day, he decided to do it himself. Number four all over. He only did it once and had to wear a hat for two weeks to cover up the mess he made.

"We already have a hairdresser appointment at four, you know that. Stop teasing me, I have been looking forward to it all week. Some quality time with my daughter." Maria tore at the pancakes as she dipped them in the sauce.

"We do?" Maria was genuinely shocked by what her mother had said. She had no recollection that today she was supposed to be with her mother.

"Yes, for the charity dinner tonight." Carly finished serving the pancakes and sat with her daughter at the counter.

"What charity do?" Maria was looking directly at her mother. Nothing was registering with her about a charity function.

"Maria, we discussed it last week. It was for the Heart Foundation. You know how much your father liked to support them. You said you would come with me? You told me to book the hair appointment for us both?"

"I did?" It was coming back to her now but she didn't let on to her mother. With everything that had been going on, a ball was the last thing that had been on Maria's mind.

"Yes, you did, that is probably why you have nothing in your diary. And now you have told me you have nothing in your diary it's still a date." Carly smiled at Maria. She knew she had her. Maria was going.

"Then I am only eating one more pancake, if I need to fit into some cocktail dress." Maria pushed the rest of the pancakes towards her mother.

"Okay, it's a deal. Why don't we go dress shopping this morning. Will be nice to have something new to wear. Spend some quality time together. You have to look your best, you never know who might be there." That last sentence had Maria worried. It was the way those words trickled off Carly's lips. She already knew of someone that was going to be there. Someone with whom her mother had formed an opinion on. A matchmaking opinion.

"Mum, this isn't a blind date thing, is it? No matchmaking. We had a deal."

Carly poured them both some more coffee.

"There is no matchmaking. I was just saying. You never know who turns up at these events." Maria didn't believe her. Her mother wasn't looking at her either which always meant she was up to something.

"I mean, last week there were two princes and a king at the Hodgkinson charity ball. All without dates. I mean, don't all girls want to be a princess?"

"No, Mum, they don't. Not all girls want to be princesses." Maria was smiling at her mum. She knew that deep down somewhere she would have had a plan to fix her up. There always was.

"Oh, okay then. That shocks me, maybe that was just in my day. I suppose that women would have to settle for becoming the wife of the vice president then. Or something along those lines. Kids today." Maria spat her coffee out.

"Mum, you haven't?"

* * * *

When Alex awoke it was eleven a.m. Oliver had been up since nine, he had left the room and fetched food and coffee for the both of them.

"It's still warm." Alex grabbed the coffee off the side and sat up in bed. There was a smile across her face. As soon as they were back at the hotel she practically jumped on Oliver. They made love well into the early hours and then Alex fell to sleep. Real sleep. Oliver had laid awake for a few hours longer waiting to see if she was going to be okay. She was, she didn't move. She looked more refreshed this morning than she had in a long time. Oliver was sat at the desk with the laptop open in front of him. He had been watching the news reports on yesterday's events.

"Is there anything on the news about our friend Victor?" Oliver turned his chair around stood up and joined Alex on the bed.

"A little but nothing we need to concern ourselves with. The first reports stated it was a rival gang. Well, that's the press release anyway. They must be very concerned about keeping the Real Avengers out of the press at the moment. There is momentum behind them that the government are worried about." Oliver had kept up to speed with the news every day. It was true they were getting a cult following from all walks of life. The people had loved the justice they were dishing out.

"Besides, what with the money I took from downstairs, and it would seem the girls did a good job of clearing out all the drugs, all they found this morning were a few bodies." Oliver had filled their bag with the money from the downstairs apartment while Alex was taking care of Victor. They had made a six figure profit from last night's work. Oliver pulled the girls together and explained to them they weren't real police. There had been seven girls there last night and they all left with drugs worth six figures also as a start to a new life. Oliver wasn't convinced they would change their ways.

"Funniest thing so far this morning though was Victor's family, they are claiming he was kidnapped as to explain why he was there. I am sure they will be able to cover the whole thing up given the money they have."

"I suppose it is going to be hard without Christopher's help?" Christopher Mellor had been following in Alex's footsteps as she took care of the mess he had created. Christopher had been capitalising on the grief by covering up the events for the grieving families. Money and power came at a price and if there was either to be made he would have been there. Until Alex took care of him.

"Yes, I suppose so. One of the working girls has come forward in a tell all fashion though. Probably to see if she can get some hush money from the family." Alex sipped at her coffee. Oliver passed over to her a tray of donuts and muffins.

"How much do you think I eat?" Alex was smiling. It was good to see. These were the best days for both of them.

"I know how much you eat. I have another three of them in the mini bar, this was just for starters." Alex laughed and tucked straight into the food.

"What was his number in the end?" Oliver knew it was good to keep Alex talking about the case. It kept her alive and it kept it fresh in her mind. She was going to be good for a few days. He wanted to make the most of that before the darkness fell again.

"Seventeen. It was more than the police had thought. You wouldn't believe that he tried to pass himself off as a gangster. He was a highly educated man. His accent did make me laugh though. All, do you feel me? and fam? Who says fam? I presume that means family, right?" Alex was chuckling to herself as she ate.

"I think it does. No idea what feel me means though? Maybe do you know what I mean?" Oliver was smiling back at her.

"I have seen it on TV. Just never heard anyone use it before. I am sure they will work out who all seventeen are? Didn't really feel like he was going to give me a blow-by-blow account. Or the girls, the girls probably knew everything. Amazing what these girls actually know. Must be an odd profession, can't say I could do it… err, yuk. Although I did dress up once as one. We were working a case in." Alex stopped as she remembered the case. She remembered Chris Masters, James Winters and Paul Simpson. She knew all three were dead now. They had been her whole backup team on that case. Oliver sensed this. He didn't want this line of thought continuing, as thinking leads to questions which he wasn't ready to answer, especially around Chris and James.

"So what plans for today, Alex?" Alex took a moment before answering and then as if a light bulb moment had happened she was back in the room and focused on Oliver.

"The beach. I want to see the sea. Just to feel the sand under my toes." Oliver turned back to his computer. That sounded a perfect way to spend the day. Although he was still worried about the message from James. He didn't want to kill Alex's mood, not today. He knew that James had held back as long as possible for him and they were going to have to deal with the Mellors at some point. But not today. Today was going to be for them.

* * * *

Maria sat on her phone in the dress shop as Carly went through every dress on the rack. She knew her mother's choice was going to be the perfect dress. It always was. Her taste was so much better than Maria's. Her phone rang just as Carly was pulling out a stunning red dress. Maria held up her hand and went to stand outside. It was James.

"It is about our friends. I think they are in San Francisco?"

"Really? What makes you think that?" Maria watched as her mother picked out some more dresses, gesturing through the window. Maria continued to point at the red one. That was the one for this evening. Especially if the vice president was going to make an appearance. Maria would make an appearance of her own. Although she didn't want to seem too keen to her mother.

"A friend of mine works in the police department there. They have CCTV images of the last people walking into the Victor Mellor's building. A man and a woman. Twenty minutes later they exit. Another fifteen after that a group of women leave carrying bags and suitcases. They believe that they were hookers carrying drugs and money."

"They are sure it was them?"

"There was a file. They haven't released that information yet. But it is them. It had seventeen written across the top. That is Alex."

"Do you know where they have gone now?"

"No, but I have sent some of our men to San Francisco. We will get access to all the footage and road traffic cameras. I have paid our way. They will find them, Maria."

"Good. Let me know when it's done. No matter the cost, James. James, you know what I mean, don't you? By when it is done?"

"Yes, Maria." James had no choice but to tell her. His friends in San Francisco had given him the heads-up. They were going to announce it was the Real Avengers later this evening. By telling Maria it had meant he was ahead of the game and she was going to trust him.

"Good." Maria hung up the phone. She froze. Saying the words was easy. She was aware the type of people that worked for her father. She was aware of their capabilities and what they had done for him, for all of them in the past. Michael had ensured they kept busy cleaning up mess. The words were easy. How it made her really feel wasn't. After a few minutes, Maria headed back into the store to try on the red dress.

Chapter 4

"Dad, we didn't even see Alex when she came back from Italy. It was months and this woman, this woman has seen her. She only lives twenty minutes away? Why would she confide in her more than us? She knows something. I don't know what, but she knows more than she is telling us." Jason took another beer from the cooler as they sat on the porch. Over the last few months the stockpile of beer had diminished in his father's house as they sat on the porch most days trying to make sense of what had been going on.

"If you feel that way, and I trust you, Jason, then we need to bring her in. Let's try to do this by the book." Jason knew his father was testing him also.

"I know, Dad, but for what? Being Alex's friend? She is not withholding evidence really as we haven't been honest with her. We haven't even listed Alex as missing?" He passed the test. Fred needed to take the emotion out of this and try to keep both of their heads clear.

"Your sister is missing though, Jason. Maybe it is time that we did? Whatever she is doing, secret mission or not, this can no longer go unanswered. Someone somewhere will know something? Your mother is going crazy with worry about her. I am playing it down but she doesn't believe me any more. She reads the papers as much as I do. I know she thinks that is her." Fred knew that registering her as missing was going to get them removed from the investigation. It was protocol. That was why they hadn't done this so far. This was his daughter. He needed to find her and bring her home.

"I know, Dad, but I, we need to find her. Give me till Monday night. I have arranged to meet with Jack's father Monday morning and then I will go back to Mrs Quaid. I will tell her everything, and see if that gets me any more information. If I have no joy, then Tuesday we register Alex as missing. Then we can interview Mrs Quaid formally." There was a silence. Jason waited for his father to respond. As pushy as Jason was, he would always take his steer from his father.

"I wonder if we shouldn't register her as a person of interest instead?"

"What? What do you mean a person of interest?" Jason was out of the deck chair and standing up to his father. Fred knew that was going to get a reaction.

"Hear me out, Jason. Missing people are not top priority for any police force. You know this. If we register your sister as a person of interest for the Curle case or the Real Avengers, any case really. Then statewide troops will have her in their sights. It will be quicker and easier to find her. If she is working with a secret mission team it makes no difference anyway? If she has that type of clearance whatever she has done she will have immunity." Jason couldn't fault the logic. He knew his father was right. They would find Alex a lot sooner if they did this. Still the thought of registering his sister as a person of interest in a crime didn't sit well with him.

"But, dad, are we really going to let someone arrest Alex? That's what they will do at first. They will all think she has done something? What if she resists? What if things get out of hand?" Jason knew that happened sometimes. Even he had over-enforced his hand at times arresting someone. The thought of someone doing that to his sister was a lot to take in.

"I don't care what people think, Jason. I just want her home. We can deal with the rest after that. Once we have her we withdraw the interest, and let her and her new friends do the rest. She is still good police, Jason. They won't do anything. I am a captain, Jason. That has to stand for something in all of this. People will respect that." Fred put his hand on Jason's shoulder.

"Alex is the innocent party here." Even though he said those words Fred was doubting them. As Jason heard them, so was he.

"We will put her as a person of interest. Find her, and clear this all up. This is Alex, she will have all the evidence she needs to clear her name, you know that. Whatever she is doing, you know it will be for the right reasons." They both knew that Alex would have covered herself. No matter who she was working with. Although the longer this continued, the more doubt started to creep in to both of them. Jason nodded in agreement.

"But not till Tuesday, Dad. Give me till Tuesday. I think we will get some traction after I meet with Mr Quaid."

"Tuesday is fine, Jason, let's hope that you do. Let's hope you do."

They each took a beer from the cooler and headed into the kitchen where dinner was being prepared. They both knew it was enough shop talk for one day. There were other members of the family that they needed to pay attention to.

* * * *

"Stop fidgeting in that dress, Maria. You look beautiful."

"Mum, it was too tight. It looks great, but I can hardly breathe in here." The limo arrived outside the library. Maria and Carly exited the car onto the red carpet. There were a few paparazzi snapping people as they entered.

"That's better. I can breathe now. I just can't sit down all night. I am sure that will not be an issue." Carly gave a smile to her daughter. She put one arm around her as the press took photos.

"Get you, Mum? You hate people taking photos."

"Your father hated photos, Maria. It was never me. Besides, who wouldn't want a photo with you in that dress?" They continued to walk up the steps and into the great hall.

"Damion Charles is actually speaking at this event, Mum. You told me, intimated to me, that he was likely to be a guest?" Maria noticed the posters on the wall in the entrance area as they walked through. The Michael Mellor Foundation had also managed to get a mention on the poster. Right across the top of it.

"Is he? I hadn't noticed, dear. He must have the same taste in charity as you and your father. That's nice isn't it, dear? To have something in common." Maria didn't believe a word that was coming out of her mother's mouth now. This was feeling more and more like a set-up. As they entered the great hall the floor was covered in socialites and dignitaries. This was not a normal charity event; the money in the room alone could have bought a continent, cured cancer and given everyone in the world a heart bypass. They stood at the top of the stairs and looked down on everyone swigging champagne.

"Pretty impressive, eh? We have been working really hard to pull all this together. It should be a great night." Carly was watching the room.

"It looks amazing, Mum. I am not surprised, you are great at this. Must have been hard to arrange to get the right speakers though." Carly didn't rise to the bait. She simply gave her daughter a smile. They were greeted with champagne and both took a glass as they descended onto the floor. There were a lot of polite nods and gestures as they walked into the crowd. This circle of people were familiar faces to the both of them. Money interacted with money. Christopher always taught his children that. To get ahead, you stick with your own level in society. Maria could see through the crowd there were various members of her Institute's board in the room.

The board was kept as a secret board. The work they were doing was never to be discussed in public or in private with anyone else other than the board itself. It was the reason that initials of the members were only ever used in the minutes of the meeting. Wherever they could, they left no trace to be uncovered. Maria nodded at each member as she passed but didn't stop to engage with any of them. Somehow Carly had manoeuvred them to the front of the room. There was a diagram in front of them with the seating arrangements. Maria headed over to it. They were on table one. It wasn't a shock to

Maria. The fact she was sitting next to the vice president also didn't come as a surprise. She looked over at her mother as she surveyed the room. This was a set-up. Maria knew it but she couldn't quite find herself to be upset with the plan. An evening with Damion Charles wasn't something she would have turned down. Even if she had been asked.

* * * *

Oliver lay watching as Alex slept. This had become one of his favourite pastimes especially when Alex was at peace. It was a drive but they had walked on the beach. Alex had felt the sand between her toes while eating ice cream. They came back to the hotel and made love. Alex immediately fell asleep afterwards. Oliver had the sports centre on low on the TV and Alex was laying across him. This wasn't going to be the end of the night; as soon as she awoke they would go out to eat. Her appetite was back and while it was, he would ensure she was full. He just didn't want to disturb her. He picked his phone up off the side, and returned the text to James. One word. Cure.

James had been standing in the library. Not on the floor with Maria and Carly but on the first level watching over them. He wasn't the only security there this evening. There was more security than guests. Each following their marks, every movement. James replied one word in return. Monday. Maria had a meeting planned for Monday. There were high hopes of the breakthrough. Christopher Mellor had alluded to this the night that he died. The night that Alex found out the truth about what he had done to her. Oliver was going to cure Alex. He was confident of it. That had to become his main focus now. Alex started to wake. Oliver ran his fingers through her hair as if to sooth her. Her eyes closed again and he went back to watching sports centre.

* * * *

Maria and Carly were seated for dinner. The vice president hadn't arrived yet. At the table were the other organisers of the charity event. Carly knew every one of them. There was a time when Maria would have been planning everything with her mother. But with Michael's last days, the club and now her father's work, she had lost touch with her mother's colleagues and their latest exploits. Something they were all keen to talk about with her. Carly interrupted to try and remind her daughter why she was here tonight.

"He is due to speak before the dinner, Maria, so he will be here soon."

"Thanks but I didn't say anything, Mum? I am not particularly interested when he will arrive. I am more interested in how you managed to get him here in the first place? And whether this is a set-up from you or both of you? Does he know I am coming? Did you invite me as his date?" Carly smiled and went back to her conversations around the table. Maria checked her phone to see if there had been an update on San Francisco. There wasn't. She sat looking at her phone. It had been an intense few months since her father and brother had gone. She never realised how much she had depended on them. With Michael there was always something to do, somewhere to go. They were the faces around town. No longer was that the case. Maria had thrown herself into work as a distraction but it was times like this she missed her brother to talk too. Two men appeared at the table bringing an extra chair and moving cutlery around to make an extra space.

"Excuse me, gentlemen. What is going on? Why are you laying another place at our table?" Carly was not happy.

"Sorry, Mrs Mellor. It was a call from the vice president. He is bringing someone with him. He has asked that they sit at the table with him also."

Maria looked at her mother. Not quite what she expected. Not the matchmaker she thought she was.

"Who is this person that he is bringing?" Maria could tell that was her mother's serious voice. If it was a date, then that was going to turn her plans upside down. This whole event had been organised by her mother for the sole point of getting the two of them together.

"I am not sure, Mrs Mellor, they didn't say. They are five minutes out. So he is due to address the room shortly. I am sure you will find out then." The waiters disappeared almost as quickly as they had appeared.

* * * *

"I swear to you it is true. The first time my father went to a Chinese restaurant. It must have been a turnip or something but the carving was amazing. Looked exactly like a swan. He just broke off the wing and dipped it into the soya sauce. They went mad. Jason and I were peeing ourselves. Jason has been dining out on that story ever since. Not often you get one over on my dad." Alex sat opposite from Oliver at the table. Oliver listened with intent, she was so happy, full of life. So different than the person she was twenty-four hours ago. Whatever they had done to her at the Brown Institute had been nothing more than criminal. This was the real Alex. The person he knew that she could be again. This was the person he fell in love with. She was now the woman behind the woman. But he would get her back.

"Jason explained to the manager in the end that he had told Dad to do it. Cost us another twenty dollars but it was worth it. So how about you, Oliver? Any funny Chinese stories to tell? They don't have to be food related. They don't even have to be Chinese." They had already ordered. Alex ordered sweet and sour chicken balls, rice and chips. This had been her stable diet for three months after Paul had died, but she was actually the person to recommend what they were going to eat. She was hungry. The duck and pancakes to start with had been new. Adventurous, Alex had called it when they ordered. The donuts from this morning. Hotdogs and ice cream at the beach and now this. This was more food than Oliver had seen her eat in a week.

* * * *

"Madam President, this is indeed an honour." Carly shook the president's hand as Maria and the rest of the table stood up. Damion Charles walked directly to the podium. Throwing a glance in their direction as he did.

"Sit down, please. Sorry to gatecrash. I was talking to Damion earlier this evening and he told me of his plans. I thought it such a worthy cause in great company I would be a fool to miss it." As the president said great company, she was looking directly at Maria. Maria had a nervous feeling that she was the real reason the president was there. Victoria turned her chair to face the podium and sat down. Damion stood and delivered his speech. The room had been captivated. It was clear he was a natural at holding the room. Just the right balance of laughter and serious message about the charity and its worthwhile endeavours. It finished to a round of applause and a standing ovation for Damion. He thanked them all and then joined the president and Maria at the table.

"That was outstanding, Damien. Thank you so much for doing that."

"Thank you, Mrs Mellor. I am honoured that you asked. It is such a pleasure to see you again." Mrs Mellor had been a familiar sight to Damion. Long before the campaign trail, the Mellors had been regular visitors to the Charles household. Maria heard the words I am honoured that you asked. Confirmation that this was all her mother's doing. Damion greeted everyone in turn leaving Maria till last.

"I am sure I have seen you before, Miss Mellor." He smiled as he sat down next to Maria. Maria felt as if the dress she was wearing just got a little bit tighter. It was that or she had indeed lost a little breath as they shook hands. She couldn't remember a time that she had been in his company without Michael, and Michael always stood out in the limelight. Now was Maria's turn to stand out in the crowd.

"So what is for dinner this evening, ladies, as I am starving?" Damion grabbed the menu from the middle of the table and everyone returned to their conversations. He read through it and then turned his attention to Maria. Carly watched as he slightly adjusted his chair in her direction, smiling as he did. He leaned over and whispered into her ear.

"I just wanted to say I am sorry to hear about Michael. He was a good friend, and your father. Both great men. Taken far too soon." He leaned back. He didn't want to keep invading her space. Maria wasn't expecting it. But he smelled good. She heard the words, but it was the smell that lingered.

"Thank you." Maria practically mouthed the words rather than saying them out loud. It was a good start. He had addressed the elephant in the room and now they could move on with the evening. There was something about Damion Charles, an inner strength and purpose. Most military men that had seen action were comfortable with conflict. Damion Charles was comfortable with everything. A table of women in front of him and he had managed to charm each of them with a single smile.

"Ladies, you have done an amazing job with the library. The decorations are just wonderful, you can hardly recognise the place. I don't know how you all find the time. I certainly know who to call now should I need some assistance with my new house." There was a chorus of thank yous from the table as the food started to arrive.

"This looks delicious, Mrs Mellor. I will warn you though, I am more of a burger and beer type of guy." There was laughter from the table. Damion Charles had won the hearts of the nation through being honest and straightforward. On the campaign trail he had been the face of the common man. His plate arrived with a silver dome across the top and was placed in front of him. He looked around the table and lifted the lid. Underneath was a burger some fries. A bottle of Budweiser appeared over his shoulder and was placed next to him. There was another round of applause led by Damion Charles.

"We do our homework, Mr Vice President. Hope you enjoy."

"Mrs Mellor, I am absolutely lost for words. You certainly do. I didn't even know that these people delivered. My favourite beer also." Maria was looking directly at her mother. She knew how to make a lasting impression. All this time she thought her father was the brains of the operation. She was beginning to doubt that now. Carly Mellor knew how to play the room with the best of them.

* * * *

"I am absolutely stuffed now." Alex flopped onto the bed in the hotel room and kicked her shoes off.

"I am not surprised. You ate practically all of my ribs, along with your whole dinner." Alex laughed as much as she dare with a full stomach.

"I know… I am sorry, I was hungry. Beside, we share everything now, don't we? The waiter must have thought I had never seen food before. Besides, you work for me now, whatever is mine is mine, whatever is yours is mine." Oliver kicked his shoes off too and laid next to Alex.

"So I work for you now, do I?" Oliver was laughing too.

"Should I put a movie on for you, boss? A massage? Fetch you some wine?" Oliver turned to face Alex.

"When I say work for me I mean, no, I mean work for me. A movie and a glass of wine sounds perfect. If you are lucky later I may even give you a bonus." They were both smiling as Alex spoke.

"But first you need to tell me what's bothering you. You seem a bit distant at times this evening?" Alex could tell something was playing on his mind. Today more than ever. Alex was alert and on her game. Something that only happened after she had dealt with a case. Oliver had tried his best to hide it but the Mellors had been on his mind.

"You can tell me, Oliver, how close are they?" Alex took a stab in the dark that this was what was worrying Oliver. Oliver paused before he answered. He was mindful of ruining the day. He also knew it was easier to talk to Alex now, easier than when she started to slip into the darkness of what had happened to her.

"They are closer than I would like, Alex. James is still helping but there is only so long that he can hold off from finding us. He is good at his job. It is why I recruited him." Alex sat up on the bed.

"Then we face them down, Oliver. How hard can it be? Christopher and Michael are gone. There is only Maria and her mum left." Oliver had been keeping secrets, Alex didn't know about Maria, but it was time for him to bring her closer into the real world.

"They won't negotiate, Alex. Maria has taken over the family business. I mean the whole family business. Including the Institutes and the direction of the board. She is now the CEO. She is now running the Mellor household and you, we are probably its biggest threat to security. I know what I would do in her position." The way Oliver spoke, Alex knew what he would do also.

"Maria is running the business? I don't see her doing that? It is not in her nature. Hell, it is not in her DNA."

"Alex, James gives me the impression that she is anything but sweet. She has given the order for them to deal with us, if you know what I mean. And we are not the first. In her couple of months in charge she has already had half a dozen people dealt with at least. People who in the past had been opposing her father and people who were casting shadows across their name. Especially after the fire at the Henderson house. Nothing has been said about that if you think about it? She covered up most of the press. We can't underestimate her, Alex. She is becoming a formidable force and seems she is getting stronger every day." Oliver was sat next to her on the bed now. Holding her hand. Which meant it was serious. She could tell he was worried.

"Then we take the fight to her, Oliver. We can't survive doing this forever, can we? We will end up caught by the police, the secret service or worse. They are not really going to understand the work we do is for the good. Let's take the fight to Maria and give her the choice. Kill or cure, isn't that the saying?" Oliver held her hand a little tighter. Alex was strong.

"There is something else. Talking of cure… James has been tracking the progress on the cure for your condition. He thinks they are close. He thinks there will be a breakthrough on Monday." Alex squeezed his hand back as hard as she could.

"That is great, no, that is better than great. All the more reason to take the fight to her. We have the evidence. We have the tracker, the hard drive. We have all we need to prove to

Victoria what has been going on. Maria isn't going to want that to happen. We get the cure. We then bow out and she can pay us to do so. They have offered me that before, and if they don't? If she doesn't want to play ball, then we take care of Maria Mellor. If you know what I mean. She is still a Brown Institute baby and it would seem DNA isn't stopping her from killing people." Alex was smiling back at Oliver now. That was the first time he had heard Alex talk of getting out. Alex had had a good day. She could see for a while today the kind of life she could have with Oliver. It was something she never thought possible. Oliver felt a weight lifted off his shoulders. This was the Alex he wanted in his life full-time. This was why he was dealing with the other Alex so well. There was hope and Alex had just confirmed that to him.

"I always know what you mean, Alex." Alex kissed Oliver. Gentle at first but a kiss that was only leading in one direction. There was going to be no film tonight.

* * * *

"You are not a bad dancer. For a soldier, that is."

"Thank you, Miss Mellor. You are quite light on your feet as well." Damion continued to waltz Maria around the dance floor.

"I think you can call me Maria as you have your hand around my waist. I am surprised though, the fact that I was last on your list to dance with this evening. Have you seen this dress?" Maria tried to keep eye contact with the vice president as she spoke, but it was proving difficult. She would easily give her emotions away, no matter how strong she sounded.

"I was in fact saving the best till last, Maria. Besides, I didn't dance with the president... well, not yet." Damion kept her stare and smiled back at her.

"Oh, so I am second from last. You really know how to make a lady feel special, don't you?"

"I don't think anyone could ever place you second in anything, Miss Mellor." This time Damion ensured that he was looking directly at Maria when he spoke. There was almost a minute's silence before Maria acknowledged the comment. She knew it was a good response.

"That was a good line."

"Thanks. I thought so too... Not sure where it came from. It just blurted out. I was going to say something about the dress but it was a little rude." The vice president was chuckling to himself as he spoke.

"Really, something makes me think you have an armoury full of one-liners."

Damion just smiled and carried on dancing until the music stopped. He bowed and escorted Maria back to the table. Carly was smiling as if she had woken on Christmas morning. She had followed them dancing all the way around the room. Carly knew her plan was starting to come together. Maria tried not to look at her.

The president was looking directly at Maria when she returned. Over dinner she had hardly said two words to Maria but she was drawn into her gaze more than once. There had really been no need for the president to be there. Maria knew she was only there to watch her. To let her know that she was close. There was something going on behind the scenes. Maria was sure of it. The president had been looking into her father.

She had already told Maria that. Maria knew her attention had now changed to her. She needed to prepare herself for that.

"Ladies, we must leave. It has been a great honour to help support your amazing cause. Mrs Mellor, thank you so much for the burger and the beer. I must say that was a first for me. A great surprise." Damion and the president said their goodbyes to all of them. Victoria ensured Maria knew that she would see her again soon. Maria was last again for Damion. He shook her by the hand and gave her a kiss on the cheek. She had been the only one to get a kiss. Carly was happy, she classed that as a success. They left the table in a buzz of excitement over the evening. When nobody was looking, Maria looked at the piece of paper Damion had placed in her hand when they shook. It was his private number, and a message saying call me anytime. She quickly placed it in her purse before her mother caught sight of it. Maria sat back in her chair. The red dress had been a good choice. She still couldn't breathe. But it was a good choice.

Chapter 5

"Hi, Mr Quaid. My name is Detective Jason Keaton. We spoke on the phone on Friday?" Jason ensured he mentioned his full name. Today he wanted Mr Quaid and Dee to know who he was. Hopefully this would help them open up to him.

"Ah, yes, come in, come in." Jason followed him through the door into the hallway and then turned right into the front room.

"Can I offer you something? A hot drink perhaps?"

"No, I am, fine Mr Quaid. I won't keep you long. I just have a few questions." Mr Quaid beckoned to Jason to sit down. Jason sat on the sofa and Mr Quaid in his chair.

"So, detective, how can I help you? Something to do with my son, you said?" Jason paused. He had said that. Just to get the meeting.

"I want to be honest with you, Mr Quaid, this isn't really about your son's case. Well, I don't think it is. To be honest, I don't really know. The thing is, I am looking for my sister." Jason leaned forward again. His body language skills hadn't defused Dee. He was sure it would work with Mr Quaid.

"Your sister?" Mr Quaid was taken aback at that point.

"Yes, my sister. Alex Keaton. She has been missing for months now and I am really concerned. She was the lead detective on your son's case. It was her last case. Since then she has been missing. I say missing. She has been involved in something outside of her job and her home and we are all worried. It isn't like Alex to not communicate with us." Jason spoke from the heart. He listened to himself as he spoke. He was confident it would get a reaction.

"Dee, never mentioned…" Jason's plan was working.

"You spoke with Dee Quaid, sir?" There was a look across Mr Quaid's face as if to say he didn't mean to say that. Mr Quaid didn't respond. He was still trying to think of an answer. Dee had visited him on Saturday morning. She had told him enough to understand how important it was to keep the secret. Her last words were swearing him to secrecy. Dee hadn't known it was her family looking for her. That's why Mr Quaid didn't know either.

"Mr Quaid, if there is anything you know, I need to know. This isn't the police asking, sir. It is her brother, her family. We are so worried. We have seen her twice in six months. And both times people have died, sir." Jason was pleading with him now. Mr Quaid knew what it was like to lose someone. His wife and now his only son were dead. He only had Dee in his life and she barely visited him now. It had been a surprise visit.

"Please, Mr Quaid, anything you know. I promise it will go no further than me and my family. You will not be in trouble for withholding anything."

It was a slight threat against him but Jason thought the context would make him talk sooner. It was working Jason could see Mr Quaid was ready to talk.

"And Dee? She is not going to get in trouble? She is a wonderful woman, detective. I wouldn't want her to get into trouble." There was a quiver in Mr Quaid's voice as he spoke. Jason had him.

"No, sir, I promise. I just want to find Alex. We all do. My mother is so worried." There was a silence as Mr Quaid concentrated on his answer.

"I must admit, I didn't believe it went that far." There was an expression of relief as Mr Quaid started to talk.

"Far, sir?"

"To the president. You can imagine. It was hard enough to know, and live with what I had done to my son. What our selfishness had brought into the world. Now to know there were so many. So many. And…"

"Sir, I am sorry to interrupt, but what you had done to your son? Your son committed suicide?" Jason was worried that he was going to miss something. He had seen this a lot in his line of work. When a confession comes, it tends to come quickly. The person confessing has made the decision to talk and they are just keen to blurt it all out.

"He did. I meant about the Brown Institute and the DNA. Sorry, I must have been rambling." Mr Quaid could tell from the look on Jason's face he knew nothing of this. He didn't need to be a detective to see it.

"You have read the letter. You know about the code. Dee even said you would know this much. She spoke to the other detectives about it. The ones that were worried about your sister when she went missing? It was the other stuff that you didn't know? Is that not right? Have I got this all confused?" It was Mr Quaid's turn to ask the questions.

"Chris Masters and James Winters? Dee spoke to them about it?" Jason had his heart in his mouth. There was the connection to James and Chris. They were looking for Alex and Dee had told them the truth.

"I think so. Dee gave them the list. And your sister, Alex, she had the code. That's what she has been doing, I think. I am sure that is what Dee said. My memory isn't as good as it once was, I am afraid." Mr Quaid was rubbing his head. It had all been a little too much for him since finding out about the Institute.

"I am really sorry, Mr Quaid, you need to tell me slowly from the beginning, what is this all about? I think, you believe we know more than we actually do?" Jason edged closer to Mr Quaid.

"You are probably better off speaking to Dee's detective if I am honest; she knows more than I do." Jason felt like he was losing him.

"Sir, just what you know. I will be speaking to Dee later today for sure. It would be so helpful if I could just get what you know." There was a pause but Jason knew he was going to speak. He waited for a response as not to push him any harder.

"All I know, son, is that Jack had a theory, it proved to be true. Where he was born, where they all were born in the Brown Institute. They messed with them. I tell you, they didn't even know what that was in my day and now they can mess with it. They messed with Jack, but not in the bad way. Not like the others, I suppose that is something to be grateful for, they turned them, the others into, you know. Jack knew the code. He found, acquired the list. I haven't really pushed on

102

how as I don't want to remember my son like that. Hundred thousand at least, Dee said, I don't know if it's true or not. I haven't seen it. The president knows about it and they want to take them down. Not the president. The other people. Your sister thinks it was to do with control and money. The president, as far as I know, doesn't like the other people. I think that's why Dee had to meet her. I think that's where your sister is. It's top secret, the president has said to tell no one. Dee told me not to tell you." Jason sat back. He tried to follow the flow of the conversation. Alex was the Real Avengers. That was the one thing he was now sure of. She was clearing a mess up for the president. Or someone else. Wherever she was, she had been trying to tell them the truth all along.

"Look, you don't want to trust the memory of an old man. It was a lot for me to take in. Dee will help you get to the bottom of this. She is a good woman. She didn't know it was Alex's family looking for her, Dee even mentioned that. She mentioned how worried you must be." Jason knew Dee was the key to this. He knew she knew a lot more than she had been telling him, clearly. Once he spoke to her and told her he was Alex's brother he would know everything.

"I am sorry, detective. I just don't think I am explaining it very well?" Jason could see that this conversation had started to stress him.

"Thank you, Mr Quaid. You have been ever so helpful. I will take the rest of this up with Dee this morning." There was no pointing pushing him, it was Dee that he needed to talk to. She had all the answers. She had given some of them over to James and Chris. That was now playing through his mind.

"Thank you for your time." Jason stood to leave.

"I hope you find your sister." Mr Quaid showed Jason to the door. Jason was dialling as he walked down the path. Directly to his father.

"Dad, it is all true. Alex is the real avenger. She is mixed up in this with the president, and it all has to do with that place she visited in Germany. The Brown Institute. It's something to do with a code. Something they have done to them. I don't know what but I am sure Dee will tell me. I believe that is why Chris and James were taken care of too. They knew about this. Dee told them. And now they are dead. Dad, what if it wasn't what Alex had done that got them killed? What if it was what they found out from Dee?" Jason paused. He just realised what he had said. And where he was going.

"I have to head past Ethan's school, but after that I am heading directly to Dee's house to get the full story. She has met with the president also. I knew she knew everything. I just knew it." There was silence at the end of the phone. It had been a lot for Fred to take in in such a short time. This had been Fred's biggest fear. That the government was really involved. Thirty years as a police captain had taught him that if they wanted something covered up, they knew exactly how to do it. If it involved the president, it was likely to be at any cost. They were about to poke a bear with a stick.

"Be careful, Jason. If the president knows, then we don't know who else is in on this. This is a lot more dangerous than we thought." Jason could sense the concern in his father's voice.

"I will, Dad, don't worry, but we are finally getting somewhere." He hung up the phone. There was a spring in his step as he headed to his car. For the first time in a while it felt like they were close to understanding where Alex was and hopefully getting her home.

* * * *

"Break it down for me in layman's terms, doctor. I am not completely sure what you are talking about." Maria sat at the head of the boardroom table. Three doctors were sitting down the left-hand side and another was standing at the podium with a PowerPoint presentation behind him. For the past thirty minutes they had been giving Maria an update on the cure.

"If you look at the curve again, Miss Mellor, you will see as the adult reaches puberty, their emotions start to become stronger from sixteen to eighteen. Others who have had the treatment, later in life they experience the symptoms a lot quicker. Sometimes days, sometimes weeks. Unfortunately, this treatment can only be reversed once the symptoms are fully developed. So the patients we have treated in the last zero to eighteen years would have to come of age, if you like, before we can administer it." Maria was following that part of the conversation.

"I get that part, but we now have a cure? That is what we are saying? That is why you have travelled all the way from the Green Institute in Montana to here today, isn't it?" There were a lot of glances exchanged across the room.

"We do; we do as far as we have tested it, Miss Mellor. We have tested it across a number of patients." Maria heard number of patients.

"When you say a number? What is that number exactly?" The glances were exchanged again.

"Twelve. We have tested it across twelve patients." There was a nervousness in the doctor's voice as he said this. Twelve wasn't a number that he was proud to present.

"Twelve? Is that all." Maria's voice confirmed the doctor's fears.

"Yes, twelve, Miss Mellor. To date they are not showing any murderous tendencies." The doctor wasn't comfortable with the number, or the position that he had been placed in. He had been ordered to present their findings. Nearly a billion dollars had been pumped into the Green Institute in Montana. Not just for the purpose of the cure but since Maria's rise in the Mellor empire this had become project number one.

"What are you saying? They haven't killed anyone? They could be just pretending not to be a killer, couldn't they? Hiding the fact? Worried what will happen to them? Jesus Christ, it is what I would do." This was the reaction the doctors had feared. There was a silence before the doctor at the podium spoke again. He had been looking at his colleagues for help but none of them were forthcoming.

"Yes, Miss Mellor, they could. I said it was early days. But this is based on the same technology that started the process. We believe it works. We want to do more testing over the next few months before we release the information to the wider board." Maria looked at the doctors and James standing in the corner.

"This information never goes to the main board. Do you understand that? I am the chairman now. I will decide what they need to know and when they need to know it." All of the doctors nodded in unison. They were in no doubt who was in charge now. A phone rang. Everyone looked at each other. Worried that this might set Maria off even more. It was James.

"Sorry." He took the phone from his pocket and walked out of the room. Five minutes later he was back in the room.

"Miss Mellor, can I have a second?" The look on James face said it was serious and that she should take this.

"Gentlemen, excuse me one second. When I return I want a timeline and a plan for this to be fixed. Am I clear?" Maria exited the room with James.

"You were right, Miss, Maria. The trace on the Keatons' phones was a good idea. I believe Jason Keaton, Alex's brother, has met with Jack Quaid's father." At the mention of the name Maria had a flashback to the club and the night she met Jack. The night he escaped the clutches of her brother. If she had let him do what Michael did best, none of this may ever have happened. Her father and brother would have both still been alive.

"And..."

"And he knew a lot, ma'am. I listened to the conversation. It was brief but apparently Dee Quaid, Jack Quaid's ex-wife, knows the whole story. Jason is going to be seeing her shortly." James paused. He knew the next point wasn't going to impress Maria.

"Maria, there was something else. Dee Quaid, she has met with the president." That wasn't what Maria wanted to hear. She wasn't surprised though. Maria knew that the president had been playing a game with her. She knew a lot more than she was saying. Maria figured that she still didn't know it all though. Victoria Owens would have acted by now if she knew it all. She would have come for Maria and the board.

"What do you want to do, Maria?" Maria knew what had to happen.

"James, you know this can't get out there. Get someone to pay Jack Quaid's father a visit, but quietly, tastefully. His ex-wife, Dee. I want to meet with her. Take her somewhere safe. Maybe the lake house. We won't be using it for a while. I need to know what the president knows. I need to know everything she knows, James." There was a tone to Maria's voice that told him everything that he needed to know. James nodded and disappeared. Maria went back to the room to continue her meeting with the doctors. As soon as James was outside he made a call for someone to visit Mr Quaid. He was going to collect Dee himself. He also sent a text. It just read 'they have the cure.'

* * * *

Alex slept in the front seat as Oliver was driving. She awoke at the sound of the text message on Oliver's phone.

"Who is it?" Oliver pulled the phone from his pocket. And looked at it.

"James. He was just checking in." Oliver wanted the cure before he said any more to Alex. The last forty-eight hours had Oliver dreaming of a normal life. Even he didn't want his own hopes raised any more than they already were. There was still a lot of distance between them and the treatment.

"Where are we?" Alex stretched her arms out as she watched the road.

"Closing in on Richfield Utah. I think we should stop for some lunch."

"I agree. Although I am not upset that we missed breakfast this morning, it was worth it." They shared a smile at each other. Both thinking about this morning's visit to the shower.

"It really was worth it. Are you sure you are okay, Alex?"

"Yes, I am fine. Why?" Alex could sense the concern in Oliver's voice.

"You were dreaming." Those were words that neither of them really wanted to hear. When Alex was at peace after a case, she never dreamed. Dreams were a sign of what was to come. She dreamed when the desires were becoming too much for her. Oliver had been listening to her as he drove. He had decided to himself that if he heard Michael's name he would pull over and wake her up. He didn't. Michael's name had become a sign for a really bad dream.

"I don't remember. It couldn't have been a bad one." Alex lied. She half-remembered the dream. It had started already. They both knew what the dream had really meant. It meant that the need for work would start to return.

Alex and Oliver had discussed a plan to talk to Maria and try and resolve their differences. To get the cure. In order to do this Alex was going to need to be in control of her functions. Something that when the hunger took over she was not. Oliver knew she was going to need a case before meeting with Maria. At least one, now given the time frame from the last case. They were avoiding travelling on main roads as much as possible. Driving, as they didn't want train or bus tickets in their names wherever they were. They never knew who was watching. But conducted themselves as if the world was.

* * * *

Jason arrived at Dee's house. His head had been spinning all morning with the news that he had received from Mr Quaid. He would have preferred to go straight to see Dee but Ethan was heading to soccer camp and he had to say goodbye to him before he left. No matter how much he loved his sister he still was a good father first.

The walk up the driveway started to concern him, he could see the front door was still open. With no other movement around the house. He walked up to the front door.

"Dee?" He pushed the front door open. The lamp by the door was on the floor. This didn't look good. Jason immediately pulled his gun.

"Dee?" The whole downstairs was open-plan so Jason had a good view of his surroundings. The rug off the back of the sofa was on the floor. He walked towards the kitchen area. There was a crunch underfoot. Broken glass. There were drops of blood on the glass also. As he reached the kitchen area there was even more blood on the sideboard. Jason reached for his phone.

"She is gone, Dad, gone and there are signs of a struggle. Some broken glass, a knocked over lamp and rug. Blood in a couple of places. Not masses of it but enough to show there was a struggle at some point." There was silence at the end of the phone.

"Did you hear me, Dad? She has gone. Dee has gone. Someone has taken her, I am sure of it. What do we do now?"

"Hang up, Jason." The tone of his dad's voice ensured that he did as he was told. Jason hung up the phone. He stood for a moment. Thinking why his dad had reacted like that. They had both come to the same conclusion. Jason searched the house. Dee's computer had gone. He had noticed it on his last visit as it was an old tower type. Most people had laptops nowadays. For someone to take that as well meant there was probably evidence on there.

There was nothing else he could do. He was going to call it in but he wanted permission from his father first. Plus, he kept looking at his phone. Something bigger was going on. All he could think was to speak some more to Mr Quaid. He didn't push him because of Dee but without her he was going to need to push harder. He needed to know everything she had said to him on the Saturday morning visit. And he needed it in clarity.

* * * *

Oliver pulled up at the diner. Diner food had become an all too often necessary for them. When Alex was well they both would discuss how they hungered for a nice home-cooked meal. One of her father's roast dinners had been promised to Oliver on a dozen occasions. They sat by the window as they always did and ordered. While Oliver ate, Alex pushed her food around the plate. With no breakfast Oliver could tell those symptoms. Lack of appetite and the dreams had started. This was the shortest recovery she had had in their time together. He didn't push her to eat. He was comforted by the point that they were at last heading in the right direction. Towards the issue rather than running away from it.

* * * *

Jason took thirty minutes to get across town to Mr Quaid's house. Walking up to the house all he could think about was how hard to push him. He was an old man but he was now the only link they knew to Alex. There was nothing he wouldn't do to get his sister back. He knocked on the door. There was no answer. He knocked again. Jason didn't like it. Mr Quaid didn't seem to be the kind of person who would have gone fishing or anywhere. Jason had imagined he sat in that chair all day watching TV. He pushed the handle to the front door. It came open. For the second time in an hour he didn't like the thought of walking into somebody else's house.

"Mr Quaid… Mr Quaid?" There was no answer.

"Mr Quaid. It's Detective Keaton. I am coming in." There was still nothing. Jason walked into the front room. Mr Quaid was still in the chair where he had left him. Just as he had imagined. His head was to one side, and it looked as if he was asleep. Jason walked over and shook him.

"Mr Quaid… Mr Quaid?" He fell forward. Jason caught him and leaned him back in the chair. He grabbed his wrist and felt for a pulse but he knew the answer before he did. There was nothing. Mr Quaid was gone. A cushion from the sofa opposite was at the side of the chair on the floor. It wasn't there this morning. Jason put two and two together, and although he didn't know it yet, he made four. His visit this morning had cost Mr Quaid his life, probably Dee's too. Whatever was going on, somebody didn't want them to know any more. Jason left the house without phoning it in. He didn't trust his phone. He didn't trust anyone but his father. That's who he needed to see. He needed to get somewhere secure. He needed to get to his family.

Chapter 6

Opening her eyes made no difference, the room was still dark. Not a shape, not a sound. She called out into the darkness but there was no response. She stood up. Her legs were shaky at best, she felt as if she was drunk or drugged. The strength that she once had was gone. She called out again. There was still nothing. She decided to try and move to find her way out of the darkness. In the back of her mind there was a drop somewhere. She shuffled her feet as close together as possible while holding her arms in all directions. It took minutes of shuffling but then she found a wall. She followed it until she found another wall and then two more. It was a cell. It felt like a cell, a square cell, it was small and there was nothing in there but her. She called out again. Still nothing. Thinking about it, there had been no door. No escape from the room. All she was able to feel were walls. Solid walls. She looked up. It must be a pit. It was the only explanation. Someone had dropped her in a pit. She shouted upwards. Still nothing. She sat back on the floor. She needed to reserve what energy she had. There was a fight coming. She could feel it. Her body had started to tingle in anticipation for it.

"I know it's you." She whispered her words. She knew now she didn't need to shout, he would be listening. He would be close. He was always close.

"At least tell me where we are..." She waited for a response. He would engage her, she knew it. He liked her to know he was there. He liked her to know he was in control. They knew each other. She knew this journey they were on; it was always going to be together.

"You know where we are." He took the bait. He was close. He was here with her although she couldn't see anything. She knew his voice. At times she craved to hear it.

"I don't, I don't know where we are." He was silent again. She could feel him close to her. Her arms were outstretched. She stood again. It felt more comfortable. If she was to be attacked she could fight better on her feet.

"What are you waiting for?" She felt a breeze as she spoke. It was hot, really hot. But a breeze meant an exit, somewhere to go to after here. Her instinct was to walk the walls again. Find the breeze.

"There is nothing else to do but wait. This is the waiting room." He spoke softly to her. There was a calmness in his voice. She knew that could change though. She had heard that voice a million times in her dreams. It never remained calm. At some point it would scream at her. At some point he was coming for her.

"What are we waiting for?" There was no response. The silence was deafening. She wanted to scream but she knew it would only play into whatever game he was playing.

"Why are we here?" She tried to keep her voice low. Like his. Calm as not to show that she was scared. The darkness didn't scare her. It was who was in the darkness that did.

"We were always going to end up here. Together. This is where we belong."

She gave into her urge and paced along the wall. She needed to find that exit. She imagined him looking at her. Following her in circles ready to attack. He probably had night-vision goggles. Laughing under his voice as he watched her helplessly stumble.

"We don't belong together." She wanted to make it clear to him. Knowing her voice was getting louder with temper. As the words left her mouth she also didn't believe herself. She knew they belonged together.

"Of course we do. We are the same, you and I." She could feel her blood boil at the sound of that.

"We are not the same, we are not the same." While her voice was raised, his remained the same. It made her want to scream even more. There was silence again. She had been through every wall twice. There was no door. Although the breeze kept coming every now and again, it was hot and getting hotter. She started to stomp her feet. Maybe there was a grate. Maybe she was in an attic of some kind. The exit and breeze could be below her.

"Just get it over with." She was shouting now. The heat was getting to her, the silence was getting to her. She bent over to touch the ground. The heat wasn't coming from the floor.

"It's not time. We will know when it is time." Whatever was coming it didn't bother him. He wasn't worried about it or scared. He was just waiting. Patiently waiting.

"Time for what? What stupid game are you playing? Michael, what are we waiting for?" His hand was at her throat as she was thrown back against the wall. She had been expecting it but still she couldn't defend it. He had her pinned up. His breath was on her cheek. She could see the eyes. The rest of him was still a silhouette in the darkness.

"For that." The heat came. There was fire everywhere, the opposite wall to where he had her pinned disappeared into a ball of flames. She knew where she was. She knew where they were going.

"Welcome to Hell, Alex. They are expecting us…" Michael licked her cheek as he said it.

Alex jumped out of bed with such a force that Oliver didn't have time to catch her. She was on the floor wiping her hand at her face. She could still feel his tongue as he licked her. She felt hot as if the door to hell was still open. It took a while for the real world to come back into focus.

"Alex, Alex, you are fine. It's me. I am here." Alex looked around the room. Oliver was kneeling over her. She jumped into his arms. He held her as tight as he could. He had known this was coming. It had been four days. He hoped for longer but whatever they had done to Alex it was taking its toll and fast. Oliver manoeuvred her back onto the bed and she lay next to him. He lay stroking her hair for the next ten minutes while she calmed down. They had managed to travel all the way to Colorado, just outside of Denver. Oliver knew this was about halfway to the Mellors and hopefully the cure. This was as good a place as any to solve a case. The one thing the board of directors for the Institutes had insisted on was ensuring that they had a hold on every state. They would purposefully seek

116

out opportunities to exploit a successful businessman. If there wasn't one, they would create one. Provide extramarital partners to wealthy older men. They would then ensure that these men found themselves at the Brown Institute. Helping Christopher Mellor and his board take a hold of the future.

Oliver knew that after this case if he found another case closer to home, hopefully that would mean he would have his Alex firing on all cylinders for the showdown with Maria.

"It is okay, Alex, I have been looking while you slept and I have found a case for us. For you." Alex turned to Oliver and smiled. She knew she needed to hear those words. She knew she was no better than the guy in the alley now. Addiction was addiction.

"It's not a big one. Well, when I say not a big one, it is one man, alone. All in all, though, he really needs to be dealt with. And quickly." There was a tone to Oliver's voice that sounded to Alex that he really meant that.

"You really believe that, don't you? Sounds intriguing. Who is it?"

"The guy's name is John Andrews. The right cocktail mixes off our list, and present when all the girls were abducted. Not that we needed the tracker for that one. It has been going on for nearly eighteen months now." Alex sat up on the bed. She knew the name.

"Really eighteen months? Doesn't seem that long. Do you know I have nearly looked this guy up a couple of times? There was always a case closer to me. I could always do good work closer to home." Alex paused at the thought of home. She hadn't thought about them for a few days but suddenly they were all in her head now. Mum, Dad, brother, family. She tried to shake it. She was better away from them. They were safer not knowing her. Chris and James had been too close and it, cost them their lives. No, the best she could do was keep away until this was resolved.

"The Cowboy, I guess that means we are near Colorado? I didn't know we had come that far?" Alex had been in and out of it for the last couple of days and hadn't noticed Oliver booking them into the motel.

"Yes, The Cowboy. I don't know why they continue to have those awful competitions though. Especially given that he has already taken six victims. The governing bodies have a responsibility to their contestants, don't they? It's not like the press haven't had a field day."

"I blame the parents. They have a responsibility. Some people don't deserve to be parents, do they?" Oliver was now shaking his head.

"No, they don't. They are creepy things anyway. Who would do that to a child? Especially your own child."

John Andrews had been nicknamed The Cowboy, not only because the way he dressed and his fascination with the Wild West but because he had been abducting girls from beauty pageants. They had always been taken when they were dressed in the cowgirl uniform. Despite the fact they knew the timing now, he still hadn't been caught. He never hid his fingerprints or the victims. The world knew who he was. The press had started a statewide campaign to ban the competitions. To no avail. Six victims in eighteen months had seen some parents also lobby against the pageants. Nothing had worked. It was each American's right to do this with their child.

John Andrews had no age preference. His victims had aged from six to eighteen. It wasn't sexual but it was violent. Each of the bodies recovered would be battered and bruised, strangulated. He then placed an arrow through the heart of his victim. It wasn't shot; it was placed carefully through the ribs and pushed in, after they had died.

Oliver had done his research and there was a pageant today. Just outside Golden which was close enough to the Motel. Four of the bodies had been recovered near Lookout Mountain and Buffalo Bill's grave. Both of these locations were a short drive from Golden. John Andrews almost had a ten-week craving. His victims were spaced out which gave the impression to the police that he was someone passing through. Given all this information, Oliver was betting The Cowboy was going to strike again today.

"We could deal with this case today, Alex. There is a pageant not far. He will strike, I am sure of it. We will be doing the world a real favour by taking care of this guy. Something creepy about the whole thing, if you ask me." Alex agreed with Oliver.

* * * *

"Dad, I haven't phoned them in. It is really weighing on me. What are we going to do? Mr Quaid is still sitting there in his chair. And Dee, I have no idea where she is?" Jason was worried. This wasn't what he decided to be a detective for. He needed to be getting on with things, but his father was worried for their safety. All their safety.

"Jason. The only way they would have known that Mr Quaid had spoken to you was if they had his house bugged, or our phones. Given our connection with Alex, I am betting on the latter. We need to decide how we are going to progress this. First of all, no more phone calls. We only talk in person and that includes at work. We also need to stop going anywhere on our own. This is serious, Jason. If they are willing to kill to protect this secret, we need to be safe." Jason knew his father was right, but now they were as worried for each other as they were for Alex.

"I will get Steve to send a car past his house. That way it is not connected back to our station house. Whoever is watching can't tie it back to us or Alex. We have to be careful now. The people we are looking into? They are dangerous." Fred had spent his whole career in the police force. Working his way up to captain very quickly. He believed in the law but also understood there were people senior to him that operated outside of it.

"What about Dee, Dad? We can't just leave her?"

"What about her? We don't officially know she is missing. We just know she didn't show to her class last night and something has happened in her house. We don't even know where to start to look for her?" Fred didn't want anyone to find Mr Quaid and report Dee missing on the same day. It would open too many questions. It needed to come from another source. Another station house. It needed to not be connected to them. They were already knee-deep in this. There was a silence.

"We know she is missing, Dad? However, we try to ignore it. The phone calls we made have highlighted her to the watchers, whoever they are? It is our fault, Dad." Jason highlighted the word we. He knew his father had picked up on it.

"I know. I will do something, maybe get a neighbour to look into it. Someone else needs to report it. I don't want anything tying back to this family, Jason. Just leave it to me." Jason knew that was the sign to drop it.

"I spent most of yesterday looking up this Brown Institute, Dad. I can't see what is up with it. It was a big business. Originally based in France and then moved to Germany. Private hospital, medical centre and research centre. Although it closed down a couple of weeks ago. The reason it stated was for lack of funding." Jason stood up and grabbed them both another beer.

"Lack of funding? Do we know where the original money came from? What is your sister's favourite saying? Follow the money."

"Not specifically. There were lots of investors. Alex said to me that she knew the Mellors invested. I believe it was how she managed to swing a visit." Jason took a breath before he asked the obvious question. They had both been thinking it but never really discussed it openly.

"Do we think the Mellors are behind this?" Fred didn't respond.

"Maybe they have Dee? Maybe that is who we should be going after? He was highly involved with the president and governments. They have the money. With money comes power." Jason was getting excited as he spoke. Finally, the words were out there.

"If you remember, Christopher and Michael are dead. Both cases, as far as anyone else would be concerned, are linked to Alex? Do we think that the mother and daughter are now behind the Real Avengers? Mr Quaid's death? Dee's disappearance? And the bugging of our phones?" They both knew that the Mellors certainly would have an axe to grind. But who would be grinding it, was the real question.

"I don't know who else it could be, Dad? If it is not them, then I will bet they are involved somewhere. They are the only people connected at all levels. Maybe they know all about the code? That's what they have been working on in the Brown Institute? That's what Alex has uncovered: the code. Mr Quaid was keen to express that something was done to them. His son and others? He was talking hundreds of thousands. That's why nobody else knows about it? Money can cover any tracks. Chris may have followed up on Alex's original theory with Dee? He was in Germany with her? That's why he was killed? The code, that's maybe why Alex is missing in action? We know she is in action? Problem is, with our two missing people, sorry, one missing, one dead, we have no connection anymore. They have left us with too many unanswered questions. If we are to have a case? And find Alex, we need Dee Quaid back. We need to know everything." Fred knew he was right. He also knew whoever was behind this was not afraid of kidnapping and murder, which, when it came to putting all his family in danger, really concerned him.

"Meeting up with the Mellors is going to mean trouble if we are wrong. You do know that, Jason. You have said they are connected at every level. They have powerful friends. As for the rest of it, it would make sense for it all to be true if we knew about this code and what it actually meant. I think we just need to tread carefully."

"Dad, I sense it is going to mean trouble if we are right too. I think we speak to Steve and get him to start on Mr Quaid. We go to the Mellors and ask if they have seen Alex? Let's look them square in the eye, Dad, and see what they say? You always said that was the only way to get the truth, Dad." Jason was using his own words against him. Fred knew he had taught him well.

"Take Roberto with you. I think we will be overplaying our cards if I turn up. At least then we can have an escalation process. Should you think they are lying or there is more to this, I can follow up after you. I feel that this could get messy really fast if not handled correctly." Jason was happy. His father and captain had bought into his plan. At least he could get on with something.

"Okay, Dad, seems like we have a plan. I will see if I can get a meeting with the Mellors."

"Try not to make it a formal one. Keep it low-key and don't play all our cards at once. Let's find out what they know. Not the other way around. If we are correct, they have been listening to all our phone conversations already." Fred was confident Jason would handle it.

* * * *

"One more time, James. I understand she knows but I just don't see why Alex would have trusted her with this? Who is she to Alex Keaton?" Maria took another sip from her coffee.

"Dee knows about the Institute, the code and the fact that this has been all to do with money and power. Your father had been playing the long game to take over the country. That is what Alex had said to her. That is all she knows. That was exactly what she told the president. They don't know about the other Institutes, the other developments that have been achieved or the work on the cure. According to Dee, Alex was adamant about the power and money. She did mention there was a belief that the board recommended key players for treatment so they could control everything. Alex hadn't broken the coded minutes though so she didn't know who the board actually were? As for why she was trusted? All I can think of is that Alex knew no one would be looking for her? Hell, we never considered her either." James had a point. Nobody had thought of Dee and that is exactly why Alex had chosen her to keep the truth safe.

"And she has told no one else? Other than Mr Quaid, and he has been dealt with?" Maria sat back in her father's chair. Working from home had its advantages, least of all she was still in her dressing gown at eleven a.m.

"Correct. Mr Quaid sadly passed in his sleep." There was a silence. Maria didn't like to hear it. She knew she ordered it, but she didn't want to hear about it.

"And what of her last meeting with Alex? When was it?"

"As far as I can tell, it was before the night of the fire. Alex had returned from Grayling. I didn't follow her. She said she was going to her parents and I met with Oliver for an update. I am sorry." Maria looked directly at him. James felt guilty that Alex had managed a secret meeting to try and take down the Mellors under his watch. He had presumed Alex had gone straight home that day.

"It is not your fault, James... She is resourceful, I will give her that." Maria sat back. The president didn't know everything at that point. But does she now? How much did Alex know now? That was the question. And who is she talking to?

"It doesn't mean that she doesn't know more, James. She, they must have overpowered my father. Given how Alex is, she would have found out more. The thing is, how much more and how much more has she told the president?" James shrugged his shoulders. Maria sat contemplating everything that had happened. She feared Alex above everything else. The board were a formidable foe. But Alex was something different. She could take down the Mellor name with the knowledge Maria believed she had.

"No, I don't think she has spoken to the president. The president would be more on our tail if she had. The president has a whiff of something. It is Alex, she knows more, I am sure of it." Maria was back to her thoughts. Minutes passed before James spoke.

"What about Dee, and what she knows?" Maria knew Dee was a liability now. She couldn't be allowed to know this much information. Alex would have known that? So why did she trust her?

"I am not sure. She met the president at the Whitehouse? That tells me she has become a player on the chessboard. Do you think the president, or Alex, is still keeping an eye on her? Do you think she is protected? By taking her, have we played our hand? Are they waiting for us to trip up?" Maria was concerned her mind had started to create situations that weren't there.

"I don't think so, Maria, or else someone would have stopped us. Don't you think? Not that she didn't put up a good fight herself. I had a glass shatter over my head as I walked in and Peter managed to get three stitches from a carving knife in the kitchen." James was trying to pull her out of the question mode. Overthinking something was never helpful. It had been a skill that Oliver had taught him on dealing with the Mellor family. Overthinking generally led to panic, and in panic were mistakes.

"True, they would have stopped us. I don't think we should do anything yet, just keep her. She may yet be of use, since she has some powerful friends now." James just nodded in her direction. Maria sat looking directly back at him. That wasn't all, she had more to say. She just didn't want to sound weak as she did. She knew what she had asked of James. She wanted the truth at whatever cost.

"Is she fit enough?" James knew what Maria meant. Dee had tried to keep her promise to the president and Alex really hard. James was an expert in his field and persuaded her to give it up.

"She will be. She is a true patriot and tried her best to keep the secrets she had been told." Maria's phone bleeped on the table. She picked it up. It was Damion. He had been texting since the dinner on Saturday night. It brought a smile to her face but she put the phone straight back down. Her attention was back on what she was doing.

Hurting someone wasn't in her nature. It wasn't in her DNA. The Institute had taken care of that. The past three months were testing the very fabric of her soul. She could give an order, she knew what had to be done to protect her mother, and her father's business interests, but she wasn't Michael. He would have been so much better at this than her.

"Good. Okay, I need to make a call." James knew what that had meant and left. Maria took a minute. Her eyes began to well up but she fought it back. This wasn't how you deal with business. Especially in front of the staff. She needed to be strong. She picked her phone back up and read the message again. She dialled the number. Wiping her eyes as she did, she took a deep breath.

"Mr Vice President, how may I be of service to you?" Damion was laughing down the phone. Maria was smiling, a conversation with him was just what she needed to stop thinking about what else was going on around her.

"Ahh, Miss Mellor. Glad you could finally fit me into your day. You don't have to use the formal approach with me, Miss Mellor. Addressing me as Lieutenant General Charles will be just fine."

"Lieutenant General, eh? Bit greedy to have two titles."

"What can I say? People just want to lavish praise and awards on to me as soon as they meet me. It is a curse."

"Some people." Maria tried to remind him things were not going to be that easy with her. Although she didn't trust herself. It had been a long time since someone showed her this much attention. Remembering back, Jack Quaid was probably the last person to hit on her at the club. Michael had a knack of managing to keep most suitors away.

"Yes, some people. So are you going to give in to my bombardment of messages? Dinner tonight? Just you and me."

Damion had a way about him. You had to like him. Maria liked him.

"Just you and me? And your army of secret service, what will they be doing while we are on this date?"

"Ok, you have me there. Me, Brian, David, Gary, Paul, Marcus and Mark would love to take you to dinner this evening. But I swear to you, nobody else. Besides, they will eat beforehand, I will make sure of it." He had confidence in himself. Maria could tell that.

"Okay, just make sure they do. Eight people on a date is a few too many."

"Is that a yes then? Good. I will pick you up." Maria almost choked at the thought of that.

"No, don't do that, my mum will have a heart attack. I will meet you. Do you know our club? Emotions? I will meet you there around nine?" Maria was keen to keep any meeting away from her mother. She didn't need pushing into a relationship. Should anything come from this, she wanted to be in charge from the beginning. Well, just after the beginning, given her mum had set her up.

"Okay, I will be looking forward to it all day. I have to go. I am a very important man, don't you know? I have a country to run."

"Oh, I know. See you then, Vice President Lieutenant General Charles, sir."

Maria laughed and hung up the phone. He had been to their club before with Michael. That was before he was nominated for vice president. The last time she remembered he had been on leave from the army. Damion and a few friends were out for a celebration. A birthday if she remembered correctly. Michael had entertained them all evening and let them drink for free. At the time Maria was more interested in keeping her eye on her brother, than on Damion. She admitted to herself there had been times she had thought about him since. And now she was about to embark on a date with him. She hadn't seen that coming.

* * * *

Alex and Oliver pulled over and parked down the road from the pageant. They were already too late. There were police cars outside the building. Georgia Kate Erickson had been missing for thirty minutes already. Oliver got out of the car and collected all the information he could from the crowd. Five minutes later Oliver climbed back into the car with Alex.

"He already has one. She is ten and small, red-headed girl dressed in a red cowgirl costume." Alex reached over to the tracker. She had intended to get there and set it up so that when he approached she would know it. They were just late. They didn't know that the Cowgirl category was going to be the first round so the contestants had come ready. The pageant organisers thought that was the safest way of keeping the event on. John Andrews only ever took them dressed like that. The contestants could arrive late and get the risk over and done with. It hadn't worked. John Andrews was lying in wait at the back of the building. The first opportunity he had, he took Georgia. The costume had been more important than the girl.

"He is travelling fast on Lariat Loop Road. Past Mines Park." Alex watched the dot beeped on the screen.

"Surely he is not stupid enough to go back to Lookout Mountain? That would be the first place the police are going to look?"

"Maybe he is. Maybe he just knows that he is ahead of the game. He is, we need to give chase?" Oliver started the car and put his foot down. They both knew this was going to be risky with the police so close. There was a little girl involved now. Without talking they both knew that they wanted to save her. Alex needed to save her. And then deal with him.

"He has a good thirty minutes on us and is not hanging around." Alex didn't want to say that it may be already too late. But she knew it could be. There had been no reports to say that he kept his victims. He had dealt with them swiftly and then disappeared again.

* * * *

Maria was still sitting at her desk when her phone rang again. She hoped it had been Damion. It wasn't. It was her office secretary. A Detective Jason Keaton had called looking for an appointment. He wanted to discuss her brother's case with her. That was all he had said. Maria knew that wasn't the truth. She knew he was fishing for answers. Maria planned to meet him in the office tomorrow. She wasn't leaving home today. Not until her date.

* * * *

Jason knocked on the captains door.

"Captain, can I have a word?" While they were at work Jason ensured he followed protocol with his father at all time. His father beckoned him in as another detective got up and left. They waited until the door was closed.

"I have a meeting with Miss Mellor scheduled for tomorrow morning. She seems to be the only one working in the family business now."

"That's good. Steve is going to follow up on Mr Quaid. I sent a few of my guys around to Dee's house in plain clothes. They threw a few bricks through her windows and ran away. A neighbour called it in, so Steve's men are now looking into the disappearance of Dee Quaid." Fred and Jason were relieved that the case hadn't gone cold. Also the fact that neither case was going to be handled by their station house.

"I will give it a few days and then I will invite Steve out to dinner. We can go out. I have searched the house. I don't believe it is bugged but I would prefer to do it somewhere public from now on." Fred wasn't going to take any risks going forward.

"I agree. I think we still need to use our phones though for trivial things? Or maybe we could do something to test the theory? Other than that, I don't think there is a lot more that we can do now, is there? I mean, other than wait for the meeting with Maria Mellor tomorrow."

* * * *

"He has stopped. His vehicle has stopped at Lookout Mountain." Alex was getting heated. She wanted to deal with the case. She also wanted to stop him from hurting the girl.

131

Alex had managed to channel her condition into her work. Being a police officer had been so important to her, it still lay at the core of who she was. That's why she was still, in her mind, on the right side of the law.

"We are twenty minutes away." They both knew what that had meant. They were just praying that it wasn't the case.

Oliver sped the car up. It was hard. The last thing he wanted to do was be tracked by the police. But there was more at stake now. Alex sat with the tracker on her lap. She held her breath, hoping that the tracker didn't move.

* * * *

"James." Maria knew he would be in earshot somewhere. Or that someone would have been and ran to fetch him. Within minutes he was in front of her.

"I am staying here for the day now. May take a dip in the pool later. So if you need to do anything this afternoon, you are free to do so." James just smiled back at her. With no family to speak of or friends outside of Oliver and the people he worked with, there was little he or any of the security team did with any time off.

"I need to go to the club this evening around seven thirty. If that is okay. Shouldn't be out later than midnight." James just nodded again.

"We then have a meeting in the downtown office at ten o'clock tomorrow. Then I want to see Mrs Quaid." James exited and left her at her desk. He returned to the kitchen where he had been having lunch with the other security team.

* * * *

"He has moved. He has fucking moved." Alex was almost screaming at Oliver. He had sped all the way. He couldn't have gone any faster.

"We are five minutes away." Four minutes later they were at the site where the van had parked. They didn't need to talk about it. They needed to see if there was anything they could do to help her. It was a small car park. No cars were parked there now. John Andrews had fled the scene. There was a small path leading down the mountain to the left-hand side of their car. Alex looked at Oliver.

"It's where he would have taken her." They were both out of the car and on the path. If he was going to treat her the same as the others, he wouldn't have taken her far into the woods. He was never worried about anyone finding the bodies. The beatings he gave were intensive, once he had his fix he would then strangulate them. Lay the body out straight and then place the arrow into the heart. She was going to be close. Oliver called to Alex.

"She is over there." Alex came running back to him. She was laid out about twenty-five yards away. Alex ran to the body. The arrow had been set in her chest and the blood from the beating was still trickling down the side of Georgia's head. Alex went to pick her up but thought better of it. Her DNA wasn't going to help them. She was dead. There was nothing they were going to do to save her. Alex didn't cry. Tears streamed down her face but she didn't cry. She got up and walked back to Oliver.

"Let's go, we need to catch up with him." Oliver didn't say anything. As soon as Alex got into the car she phoned the police and said she had spotted something at the small car park. It would have been enough to make them come running. She didn't like the thought of Georgia being alone. Alex had the laptop back in front of her. It was still tracking John.

"He has turned down Grandview Avenue. That is almost a dead end. The son of a bitch lives here?" That was all they needed. It was another ten minutes' drive to the bottom of the mountain. They turned down Grandview.

"Take a right. He is down at the end of the road." Oliver did as he was told. As he reached the end, there was a dirt track that took them further into the park. Alex nodded to Oliver he knew he had to take it. About five minutes later they spotted the van. The tracker said they had arrived.

"It is always a van." They both got out of the car. There was no idea what they were going to face. There was a small log cabin a bit further down the track which they could see once they passed the van. All Alex could think about was why hadn't he been found so far. He was so close to where he had been dumping the bodies. Probably walked that mountain every day. They walked towards the house. The fire had been lit; there was smoke coming from the chimney. It made them both think that he wasn't alone. Oliver took the back of the house and Alex went straight towards the front door. As she approached she could see him through the window, she ducked under it. He was alone in the kitchen. Looked from the outside as if he was preparing dinner. How could he live so close and nobody knew? His picture had been all over the paper. Somebody must have noticed him. He left the kitchen. As he did Alex could see Oliver through to the back of the house. He caught her eye and mouthed the words "open" to her. She tried opening the front door. It was locked. She went to the back where Oliver was.

"Front door is locked?"

"Back is open, that is what I was saying. I thought you would want to go in first." Oliver knew this was her mission. He only came along to make sure she was safe. Alex went to the door and opened it. Her gun was now out directly in front of her. She could hear someone upstairs. As she reached the bottom of the stairs, a woman started to walk down the stairs. She was dressed as a cowgirl. She could see the outfit and hear the spurs on her boots. Alex crouched at the side of the stairs so she wouldn't be seen. Alex knew this was the intended person for John Andrews' rage. Why he always took his victims dressed as cowgirls. Too chicken to take it out on the person closest to him. She waited until the woman got to the bottom step. She jumped up and grabbed her from behind putting her hand around her mouth. She was a tall girl and had weight and height on her. Alex pressed the gun into her ribs, moved it about so that she knew it was there.

"I am not here to hurt you. I am only here for John. Now stay silent, I am going to take you outside and I want you to stay there. Nod if you understand? If you scream or warn him, there will be serious consequences." There was a nod. Alex walked the cowgirl backwards out of the back door. She released her and told her to walk towards the van, her partner would take care of her. Alex turned and headed back into the house. Alex knew the feeling. The sharp pain and then the sudden drunk feeling before the darkness came. Before she hit the ground, she knew what had just happened to her. It was a good blow, took Alex almost an hour to come around. Her head was a little fuzzy and she was laying on a sofa.

"I tried waking you a few times, Alex. But I thought I would let you sleep it off. I figured they haven't found him so far, we were hardly going to be interrupted." At least that was a familiar sound. Oliver had been sitting in the chair opposite watching Alex sleep. This had become a pasttime for him. The cowgirl was tied to a chair in the centre of the room. Alex scanned the room and then jumped up off of the sofa.

"Where is he? Where is John Andrews? Don't tell me he has got away? We need to finish this, Oliver, we need to finish this…" Oliver was up as soon as Alex was. He was worried that she would bolt out of the door after him.

"Woo, don't worry, Alex, he isn't going anywhere, I assure you." There was a confidence in his voice. She knew he meant what he said.

"You have dealt with him?" There was a sound of disappointment in her voice now as she said that. He wouldn't normally do that. He knew that she needed this. Oliver was slightly upset that she even had to ask. She should have known him better by now.

"No, no, I haven't. Of course I haven't. I have left him to you." There was a smile across his face as he nodded towards the cowgirl. Alex gave her a glance, and then another. The cowgirl needed a shave. Those words seemed to linger in Alex's head as she said them. John Andrews was the cowgirl, how had she not seen that? How had she not felt that when she had her hand around his mouth? It would have felt like sandpaper.

"Holy shit. It's him, isn't it?" Oliver was nodding. Smiling and nodding.

"It is... I was standing at the window as you both walked out. As you turned, he picked up a log and smashed it over your head. I pulled my gun to shoot but it was a girl in a cowgirl outfit. I resisted it and just ran straight at her/him, whatever you want to call him. His wig came off. I put it back on for your effect when I tied him to the chair. I wanted it to be a surprise. I tell you it was for me." Oliver and Alex were now standing straight in front of John Andrews.

"I am right here, you know. Sitting right here." John was not happy about being talked about in the third person.

"Shh, we are not talking to you. I checked her/his mail. It is all to the woman. Probably why nobody knew he was here. He lives as a woman most of the time. I am guessing a Margaret or a Joanna. Am I right? He looks like a Margaret." They both had a smile on their face as they teased John.

"My name is Andrea." John Andrews almost felt proud of that fact. Alex burst into laughter. Oliver smiled from ear to ear.

"Nice to meet you, Andrea. This is Alex and I am Oliver. I am going to leave you in her capable hands. You have got this, haven't you?" Oliver was walking towards her as he said it.

"Yes. I have this." Oliver kissed her on the cheek before he left and headed towards the car. Alex was focused again. Her head was clearing. As she stood looking at him it was unnerving that he was dressed as a woman. She took off the hat and the wig. It was better, he looked more like his photofit now. She could look past the make-up. Just not the wig. He didn't really seem to be a blonde.

"I am going to ask you a question, John, and I want the real answer. How many, John?" She waited. He wasn't speaking.

"How many, John? There are the ones we know about. Hell, the world knows about. But that is never it. That is never the full story with you people. In every one of your people's past." Alex stopped. It was the way she heard herself say your people. She knew she was one of them now. So they were her people. In essence she was one of them.

"Every one of you has killed more than the world knows. You all have secrets. I want to know how many people you have actually killed?"

"I must say, dear, I really don't know what you are talking about and if you would kindly hand me back my hat and my wig, I need to finish up the dinner. A woman's work and all that." The accent that came out of John's mouth was a southern one and one of a woman. He had perfected it over the last three years as he had been living as a woman. Alex was sure she had heard that when he said Andrea. Her mind had glossed over it. Alex was glad she had removed the wig or else that voice would have freaked her out.

"I don't really care for Andrea, John. I said how many people have you killed, John?" Alex's voice was serious now. She didn't want to play his games.

"I am sorry, my dear, my name is Andrea. You must have me confused with this person called John?" Alex hit Andrea straight across the cheek as hard as she could.

"Ouch, that hurt. Why would you hit me? Why would you? I am just a little woman." John still spoke as a woman and was fake crying as he spoke. Alex hit him again. And again.

"Please stop hurting me. I have not done anything. Please." John was quite convincing as a woman. The tears were real and so were the noises. Alex kept having to take the picture that he was a girl out of her head.

"You are a killer, John. You killed and brutally tortured those girls. I know who you are, what you are. I know everything, John. How many?"

"I would never…" Alex hit him again. And again. It wasn't working. The pain didn't make him lose his grip on Andrea. That was the only thought she had. She left him tied to the chair and went into the kitchen. She picked up the carving knife from the side and took it back into the room. Walked straight up to him and without speaking she stabbed him in the arm.

"Fuck!" That was a man's voice. There was no pretence in that. It had worked. John was surfacing.

"How many, John?" She could see him trying to compose himself.

"Dear, the name is Andrea and I am really unsure why you are doing this to me." The woman's voice was back. It was cracking but it was still there. Alex took the knife and stabbed it straight through the leg. She held it there for a while and then gave it a wiggle to ensure maximum pain.

"Fuck, fuck you, bitch" Alex smiled at John sitting in the chair.

"There you are, John. I knew it was a matter of time before you showed up. Now I am going to ask you again. How many?"

"Fuck you." Alex hit him again across the face. And then again. There was blood coming out of his nose and cheek now. Alex was mindful now with the blood from the arm and leg, she didn't want him to pass out from blood loss.

"It will save you, just answer the question." Those words made John pay attention. He figured his number was up. He knew that she meant business.

"What did I ever do to you? I don't deserve this." He was now pleading for his life. It was a start.

"To me? Nothing. To those girls, too much, John, too much. Why did you do it? If you are not ready to tell me how many, then why?" John was silent. Alex hit him again and then held the knife under his nose. She had already decided that dealing with John was going to get messy. After everything he had done to those children he didn't deserve to be dealt with quickly and quietly. He had brutally and violently killed them. What he deserved was the same. There was also the fact that there was only him to deal with. Alex felt so alive doing this that she didn't want it to end. She needed her fix.

"Come on, John, I do actually have all day and nowhere to be. So I could do this all day?" She moved the knife closer to him. He didn't doubt her.

"Come on, tell me your mummy and daddy were rich, how they didn't give you enough attention. How that had turned you into a monster. How if I leave you alone you can pay me off in millions of dollars. I have heard the story so many times. You are not unique. There are hundreds of thousands of you. I know." Alex did her homework in the car on the way to Golden. Mother and father in Oil. Lots of cash and doted on their baby boy. Some papers had wondered if they had paid for him to get out of the country. Since the world knew who he was.

"Okay, I couldn't help it. I just had the urge." Alex knew that to be true. She also knew that the urge was to kill. Even in her state she knew not to kill the innocent. John Andrews had only been killing innocents. Whatever was inside him, she figured it was already going to be there. The Brown Institute just highlighted it.

"I have had the urge for so long. I tried to stop, but I couldn't. I started with hunting. It was a release. Deer, elk, bears, anything really, anything that I could take a life. That rush of knowing that you have taken a life. At first it is intoxicating and then there was a calmness about it. Knowing that you could defend yourself against anything. Knowing that you were the alpha male. That quickly turned into not being enough. So I killed my wife. I used to live over in Utah. I told everyone she had left me but she hadn't. She is under the tree in the back garden. One night I just couldn't control my temper, and I hit her. I hit her so hard that some of her teeth ended up embedded into my knuckles. She had been line dancing at the local bar. Everybody dressed in a cowgirl outfit. Drawing attention to herself. She deserved it." Alex watched him as he spoke. She genuinely believed him about the urges. It was starting to worry her. The thought that you could lose control and kill those closest to you. The fact that there was more. More escalation. She knew the time between needing a case was shortening. Was she escalating beyond her own control?

"After killing her, I ran. I knew someone would find her. State after state. Nobody did. I don't believe they have today. I got away with it. Once I knew it was capable, every time I saw a cowgirl, I had to do something about it. I needed to get them young though. They deserved it, all of them." He stopped. Alex had the urge to hit him. She wondered if he was thinking about them or what he had done to them. Whatever he was thinking, she knew that it wouldn't be a nice thought.

"Andrea helped me. She helped me see what I needed to do. She helped me understand it was a way of life. I needed them young so that it would speak louder. That cowboys, they were the real baddies of the story. That's why I have to dress as one. As my punishment. One day someone will come for me. One day. You know, for what they did to the Indians. That is why we had to show them. We had to show them what would happen now. The Indians are going to rise up and take their land back. We know it. Me and Andrea, we know that. But the government. They know it now. The arrows, they know that the Indians are coming." Alex hit him again. And again. And again. That little speech. It made it clear to her. She knew that he was nothing but a nutcase. At first she had started to believe him. The urges, the need. They were real for Alex. But now. Talk of Indians and cowboys, he had crossed the line into insanity. Alex had to stop hitting as her hand had started to hurt.

"Bitch, that was a moment. That was a moment where I was showing you the future. Your future. Our future. We need

142

to spread the word. They are coming. They are coming, Alex."
Alex plunged the knife into the other leg.

"You don't have a future, Mr Andrews. The number, or
the next knife will go straight through your heart. Trust me, I
am not kidding."

"What the fuck does it matter? What the fuck does it
matter what the number is?" Alex pulled the knife out and
stuck it in the other arm. The screams were loud but there was
no one to hear them. James was sitting in the car listening to
music. He knew what Alex was up to. She wasn't going to
need his help. Alex pulled the knife out again. She held it next
to his ribcage.

"Okay, okay, the number." Alex pulled the knife back and
stood back from John. He was working it out in his head.

"Including my wife, including my wife, fourteen.
Fourteen women." He wasn't impressed with the number.
Alex couldn't tell if it was fear or not. At the end most of them
were impressed by their accomplishments.

"Women and children?" Alex needed to be sure he meant
everyone.

"Yes, women and children, fourteen. Fourteen is the total
number." Something about the number always soothed Alex.
Especially knowing it was always more than anyone had
expected. It almost increased the justification of her actions.

"Thank you, John, or Andrea, whichever one you really
are." John could see the expression change on Alex's face.
Relief washed over her. It was a good sign.

"Does that mean that I can—" Alex lunged at John,
knocking him and the chair backwards. She plunged the knife
into his stomach a dozen times. He screamed with every hit.

She climbed off him. She stood and watched as the life and the blood leaked out of him. It took a while. There was a lot of blood. She had almost forgotten the smell of it. But now she was soaked in it. She walked over to the table where she had placed his wig and his hat. Pulling the chair back upright, she then placed them on his head. Adjusted it to make sure she looked good. He made an attractive woman other than the stubble. Alex went into the kitchen. She had seen the arrows when she went to pick up the carving knife. She brought one back and slowly placed it through his ribs and into his heart. She knew it was a fitting end to him. The parents of the families were going to appreciate that.

Alex went into the kitchen and turned the dinner off that Andrea had been preparing. She then went back to meet Oliver.

"Is it done?" Oliver could tell by the blood covering Alex that it was.

"It is. Fourteen. It was an interesting conversation between the three of us, I can tell you." Alex was glowing. There was almost an excitement in her voice.

"Let's give it twenty minutes and call it in." Oliver looked past the blood and at Alex. He smiled.

"I agree. I am so hungry. Let's go and get something to eat."

Chapter 7

Maria entered the club. It had been a few months, but nothing had changed. It still felt like home, although she knew something was missing. Michael was missing. She could almost see him at the bar. Drunk and hitting on customers. Edward, the bar manager, came around to meet her. He offered his apologies about her brother and father. He had made into onto the invite list for both funerals but didn't get a chance to speak to them. Maria thanked him and went straight up the stairs to her office. Her desk was full of paperwork. The weekly numbers had been piling up over the last few months. She glanced through them. Edward was doing a good job without her. The club had started to turn a profit for the first time. Maria smiled to herself. She thought it was no coincidence that Michael was gone and profits were up. He did like to give free drinks away. Especially to hot guys. The club had never been set up to make money. It was a joint business venture that Maria and Michael could share. Somewhere they could be together. Maria stood up and walked over to the window. She could see the whole club from her window. Michael and her would often stand and watch the guests as they arrived. People-watching. Making up stories about who they were and why they were out tonight. They hadn't done that since Italy. That was the last time Maria saw her brother alive.

The club had been a great escape for the both of them. Maria watched as the band practised and the bar team were stocking the bar for tonight's guests. The odd customer had already arrived. They had only been local traffic, as Michael used to call them, passing through on the way to another bar. The real clubbers wouldn't arrive till after eleven. Michael and Maria never liked to enter the floor till twelve. There was a knock on the door. It was Edward.

"Excuse me, I thought you might like a drink, Maria." He was carrying an open bottle of champagne and two glasses. He knew it was Maria's favourite drink and they always kept a supply chilled for her.

"That sounds like a great idea, Edward." He walked up to her desk and poured them both a glass, handing one to Maria as she returned to her desk.

"So how are things, Edward? How is Austin?" Maria sat down.

"Things are good, Maria. He is fine. Still taking a sabbatical and doesn't know his way around the hoover or iron but I love him, what can I say?" Maria gave Edward a smile.

"I have been looking at the numbers. Things have been going really well? You are doing a great job here. Is there anything you need from me?" Edward didn't want to answer the question as it could have been loaded. Yes meant he couldn't cope and no meant she wasn't needed. Either way could be frowned upon. Edward wasn't the confident one in his relationship. Austin was. Austin had worked security for Mr Mellor for a while but handed his notice in to do freelance. The money was better and there was more limelight with superstars. Austin liked that.

"I think we are doing okay? I have a good team. It's not the same without you both here." He didn't really answer. He felt that it was his best option.

"I know. I have been meaning to pop in. To be honest, I don't think I will have the time I had before as we go forward. How about I step up your wages, and you just run the place how you think? Like I said, you are doing a great job." Edward had been hoping for those words for the last six months. Before all the events with Michael and her father. He had been practically running the place single-handed since the beginning.

"You don't need to…"

"I know I don't but I think that is best for all of us. I will still be here if you need anything. You have my direct number, don't you?" Edward nodded his head in response.

"Then it's settled. I will double your salary in the morning." Maria held up her glass so they could clink them together. Edward did. He was smiling so hard it was hard to try and be professional.

"Can I ask? What brought you down here anyway, Maria? Is there something you need? I am sure it wasn't the band tonight?" Maria laughed. She knew the band. Heavy scar music wasn't Maria's thing. It was only once a month but they liked to keep the music a variety for all their customers. Some smooth jazz or eighties music would have been more to her taste.

"No, it is not the band. Believe it or not, I have a date this evening." Edward nearly spat his champagne out. He couldn't remember her ever having a date. She smiled at him as he had the shocked expression written all over him.

"Really? A date, Maria?" Edward didn't mean to sound so shocked.

"Yes, is that so surprising? It has been known? Not often, I agree. But it has been known." Even Maria had to smile at that. It hadn't been known.

"No, that is great, really great. He must be a remarkable man. Can I ask who with?" Edward was keen to know who would be able to make Maria go on a date. He had seen dozens of men try over the time they had the club but none had ever been successful.

"You can. Lieutenant General Charles." As she said the words she could see Edward processing that name through his head.

"The vice president. Damion Charles? You have a date with the vice president of the United States? And he is coming here?" Maria nodded her head at Edward.

"I hope you don't mind me saying, Maria, he is hot. I mean really hot. I mean, leave Austin and run away with him, hot." Edward knew a good-looking man when he saw one.

"He is hot? I can't say that I noticed." Maria's phone rang. He was downstairs waiting for her. He was early as well. Maria took that as a sign he was keen.

"I have to go, that is him. And his secret service party. They are downstairs." Edward gave her a smile as she exited the room. Then he rang Austin. Maria had just made his day, and he wanted to share it with him.

* * * *

Alex's mum laid a place at dinner for her. It was Tuesday, it was dinner at Mum and Dad's night. She always laid a place for her. Nobody mentioned it as they sat down to dinner.

"Roast chicken on a Tuesday with all the trimmings, you can't beat that, Mum." She smiled back at her son. He could tell there was a sadness behind that smile now. Alex was never far from any of their thoughts. The table had seen so many great nights. So much fun and laughter. Apart from Ethan, the dinner was eaten almost in silence. As soon as it was finished Jason and Fred excused themselves to the porch. They had respected the no work at the table rule. It was getting harder to do that every day.

"Is Mum okay? She seemed to take an age to lay Alex's place tonight."

"She is struggling. I think Alex actually made it worse by coming home and visiting. She promised to visit more. Then there was all the commotion at the marketplace. She has it in her head that that shot could have been meant for Alex." Jason knew that would hurt. He also knew that his sister would have contacted her if she could. She had told them it was nearly over. But that was months ago. They both feared there was no contact as Alex knew it wasn't safe to do so. With what had happened to Chris and James, and now Dee and Mr Quaid, Jason and Fred knew things weren't safe.

"Let's not dwell on it. I will look after your mother. Are you ready for tomorrow? For Miss Mellor?"

"Yes, Dad. I have done my homework. Prepared all the questions. I have kept it low-key, as you suggested. I will ensure that she does all the talking." Fred was confident in his son. He also knew he was a good reader of people. If the Mellors had something to hide, he would uncover it.

* * * *

"I can't believe this is where you take a woman on a first date." Maria took a swig from her bottle of beer. Damion stood behind the counter, needing a pizza base.

"What do you mean? You don't like my uncle's pizza place?"

"No, I think it is really nice, but not what I expected." Maria watched as he spun the pizza like a professional. He looked very comfortable behind the counter. The apron did suit him.

"What can I say? I am not a champagne and caviar type of guy." Damion was preparing the dough but he didn't take his eyes off Maria as he did.

"You are really good at that." He had surprised and impressed her with his skills.

"I should be. I worked here every summer. My father and uncle made us all work here. Me and my cousins. They didn't inherit their wealth, they had to earn it. So we all had to have a good grounding too. That's what they told us anyway. I loved it. If I didn't join the army, I would have gone into my uncle's business for sure." Maria loved the fact that he was so normal. He wasn't what she had expected. He was better. She did feel a little overdressed though, for a small pizzeria.

"So the pizza bases are ready. I already know what the crew want. I am guessing you are a cheese, tomato, pepperoni and a hint of chilli. Maybe a little piece of rocket? Not too much. But you like a little pepper."

"It seems you are really good at this. Do you need some help?"

"No, I have it. I have made some salad and some coleslaw too." Maria was impressed. He was not only cooking for her but for the secret service also. His uncle had closed early so that they had the place to themselves for the evening. She watched as he prepared the food.

"Music, I knew something was missing. I was wondering why the place was so quiet." Damion slid the last pizza into the oven and then walked out the back and picked a CD out. Jamie Cullum. Smooth jazz. Maria's heart skipped a beat. She loved Jamie Cullum. He had done his homework. For a moment she hoped he had done his homework. In that moment she thought of her mother. She could do remarkable things. Setting this up would have been easy for her. She shook it off. No, she didn't do this. Damion did.

* * * *

"How long are you going to keep me here?" Dee sat at the counter in the kitchen of the Mellors lake house. There were no answers from her guardians. The only person that had spoken to her was who she believed was the boss. James. James had spoken to her. James had hurt her too. She was nursing some bruises on her face and body. A split lip and a cut above her eye. She hadn't been touched since. The guards had left food and drinks out for her. Showed her the fridge and the toilet and she was free to roam the house. The phones had been disconnected and there were at least a dozen men on the property. Dee was going nowhere.

"I presume that I am a guest of the Mellors?" Still nothing. Nobody was speaking to her. It was her first guess but she wasn't sure. She knew Christopher and Michael were dead and Alex had always trusted Maria.

"You can at least tell me that much? If Alex was right and this is all about the money and the power? And that they will do anything to keep these things secret? Then I am in a lot of trouble, aren't I?" Nothing. Dee wasn't going to get a reaction out of them.

* * * *

"They must get fed up of sitting in those cars? You know, they have to keep the engines running at all times. Just in case of an emergency. That just sounds silly to me." Damion walked back into the restaurant after delivering pizzas to his secret service detail.

"Don't wait for me, tuck in. Pizza is either good hot, or great cold. Tastes awful lukewarm. semi-congealed, yuk." Damion went and sat opposite Maria. He had served her first. He undid a couple of more beers from the ice bucket on the table and passed one over to her and clinked the bottles.

"Cheers, Miss Mellor…"

"Cheers, so you like cold pizza? I have learned one of your secrets. That is, how do I say this without sounding too ungrateful for this amazing feast in front of us, disgusting." Maria was laughing as she spoke.

"I love cold pizza. I think more than hot pizza. We used to make pizzas to sell by the slice here in the summer. What we didn't sell, I would put in the fridge and have for breakfast the next morning. To tell you another secret. Because I am an open man. Man of the people. Sometimes I order pizza now and put it straight into the fridge so I have breakfast sorted." He smiled at Maria. She was fast realising he had picked her up, surprised her, cooked for her and told her secrets all within the first hour of their date. She knew she hadn't dated in a long while but as dates went she was sure this was a cut above the rest. Maria picked up her knife and fork. He started to laugh and picked up a pizza slice with his hands.

"I didn't know you were so posh." Maria put her knife and fork down and picked the pizza up. She stuck her tongue out at him and then bit into it. It was the best pizza she had ever tasted. He was an amazing cook. She just wasn't ready to tell him that yet.

* * * *

"Detective Keaton, Detective Valance, Miss Mellor will see you now." Jason and Roberto were sitting in the reception area of the Mellor building. Natasha, Maria's secretary escorted them through to the boardroom. Maria was at the table looking at her phone. Damion had texted her half a dozen times this morning already. He had been a perfect gentlemen last night. They shared a passionate kiss and the end of the evening in his limo and then he dropped her back at the club where James had been waiting for her. James knew he didn't need to follow, not with the secret service on her tail.

"Please, gentlemen, take a seat." Natasha showed them to the chairs and then left to return to her desk.

Maria continued to look at her phone for a few minutes. Her father had always pointed out to her it was important to start all meetings knowing who was holding the room. Maria had learned to hold most rooms. She placed the phone down and looked directly at Jason. She knew him. She had read the file that James had laid out for her. Background on the whole Keaton family. If he was half the person his sister was then she was going to have to control the meeting. Roberto Valance had a file too. But Maria wasn't worried about him. She knew that Jason was running the show as far as she was concerned. He was leading this investigation.

"So, gentlemen, how may I help you? I understand you would like to discuss my brother's murder? I am sure that is what Natasha had said?" Roberto looked directly at Jason, Jason looked at Maria.

"Yes, Miss Mellor." Jason responded. There was a silence. Maria held her hand out as a gesture to Jason to get on with it.

"Sorry, yes, first, Miss Mellor, I think I should let you know that I do know about the events in Italy, the UK and Germany That led to the tragic loss of your brother." Maria just nodded at him. Maria had given Alex an alibi and cooperated with her story to the European police. She knew all of that was now a matter of record so it wasn't going to unnerve her. She was tempted to throw into the conversation if they knew the real killer. Now that Dr Jonathan Smith had been reclassified from suicide to murder. But it was for them to talk more than her.

"In truth, the reason for the visit? It is more to do with the situation after those events that I am more interested in." Maria nodded at him again. His idea was to get her to speak but that hadn't worked so far.

"My sister, Detective Alex Keaton. I believe you know her? She has been missing for almost six months now." Jason looked at her for a facial response. There wasn't one. All the lies she had told for Michael over the years had given her the skill of deception.

"Six months... has it been that long?" There was something about the way that Maria said that that made Jason nervous. Maria knew Alex had been missing for three months and so did Jason. He had made a mistake already. He had to try and stand by it.

"Yes, six months." Even Jason knew it didn't sound that confident that time.

"Oh, I am, sorry Detective I didn't know you had not seen your sister for that long. I have seen her in the last six months, Detective, I hope that is of some comfort to you." This was more of what Jason had been hoping for with regards to talking. Although she was a lot more confident than he had expected.

"Yes, I understand she was helping my father on her return from the United Kingdom. I am not sure what with. She came to the house about three months ago? I only spoke with her briefly to thank her for all she had done to help with my brother. Strange, she told me she had been home to see her family? For a couple of days, if I remember?" Alex hadn't told her that. Oliver had in his report. Up until the night of the fire Oliver had sent regular movement updates to her father. Which she now had possession of.

"Yes, sorry, I forgot to mention, she did come home that one night. It was brief and she just informed us she was working a case. Nothing else." Jason couldn't almost look her in the eye at that point. He was keen to try and point out that at this point they knew nothing. It wasn't far from the truth.

"The one night? I thought she was back a week later as well? A week after she visited my father and I, I am sure I read something in the news about her and a shooting in a local market? Wasn't she shopping with your mother at the time?" This wasn't the start Jason was hoping for. He had underestimated Maria. She was running rings around him.

"That was a misunderstanding, Miss Mellor. My sister didn't shoot anyone." Jason bit, he didn't mean to but the thought of pinning that shooting on his sister had riled him.

"So I heard, Detective, so I heard. Professional hit, I understand, on her partner or ex-partner? I forget. But it is good to know that at least your mother was seeing your sister on a regular basis up until that point." Jason had the feeling that Maria didn't forget anything. And knew everything.

"So, to get back to your point, Detective, you say she has been missing, with all that taken into account, for around two and a half to three months, is that correct?"

"Yes, Miss Mellor. About three months." Jason knew she had just taken a lot of his thunder away.

"So about the same amount of time between her return from the UK and seeing you. When she was just working? Are you sure she is not just taking a long holiday somewhere? I know she likes to travel. She did tell me she loved Italy." Maria was playing with him now. Jason knew this. He just shook his head to tell her that wasn't the case. He didn't really have an answer for her.

"Then I am sorry to say, Detective, but I can't help you. I haven't heard from her during that time either. Not that I would have had any reason to. Not since, well, since around the same time that somebody brutally murdered my father and the Secretary of State's son? Oh, and half a dozen people also, then poured petrol over the bodies and burnt the house down. I do hope she is all right?" Jason knew what she was getting at. She gave him a little time to process those thoughts. That is exactly what he was doing. Trying to work out his next question.

"So, as you can see, Detective, I am not sure how can I be of help to you?" Jason wanted to say, are you sure you have not seen my sister. But it felt a little redundant now. She had shown him she was up to date with the events over the last six months. She was also prepared for him.

"Do you know what Alex was working on with your father?" It was a long shot. Also Maria had already expressed that she didn't. But he needed to fill the room with words.

"As I said, Detective, I don't. My father had so much going on. Believe me, I am struggling to cope in his absence. I believe, however, it may have had something to do with the Brown Institute in Germany." Jason suddenly felt like there was a ray of hope in the conversation. Maria had brought up the Brown Institute. Maria had, because she had listened to his call to his father. She knew what he knew. In order to come out of this successfully she knew she had to divulge as much of the truth to match the lie as possible. He leaned forward.

"I know she went there for him, with him. I am not really sure how that conversation went. Other than she borrowed our plane. Whatever it was that she did, I know it must have been important as he gave her resource and money. That was after the events in Italy, as you said, Detective. So I can presume that your sister and my father must have been close. I believe Oliver, one of my father's most trusted men, is still with her wherever she may be. Maybe she doesn't even know about the loss of my father. I haven't seen her since that day she came to the house. She may well think that she is still working for him?" Maria had read the file and listened to the conversations over the phone. She was keen to mention everything that they already knew. She was also keen to tell him for a second time she had not seen her in three months. That wasn't a lie. She had spent enough time looking for her.

"Do you know what the Brown Institute was, Miss Mellor?" The word "was" told Maria he had done his homework. It had only been closed a week.

"I can't say that I do, other than what I have read. It was a hospital and research centre of some kind? My father donated billions to these types of institutes around the world. He was a great humanitarian. Never really kept track of these things. Turned up for the odd plaque and award was about his limit." Jason knew all of this already. He wasn't getting anything new from Maria.

"Do you have a contact number for your father's man who is supposedly with Alex?" Jason used the word supposedly on purpose although he knew all the reports he had read for the

Real Avengers had a man and a woman involved. He wanted Maria to know that he wasn't comfortable with the answers he was getting. Although he couldn't find fault in her.

"No, I am sorry, I don't." Jason needed something to put her off balance. Nothing so far was working for him. If he could find something, she might make a mistake? If there was one to make? He was adamant there was, the truth lay behind this woman in front of him. She was just a master of keeping it to herself.

"Can I ask you a few questions about Dee Quaid?" Maria looked directly at him. He pulled out his notebook. There was nothing on it. It was just to see if it would get a reaction out of her. If she had taken Dee, it would be written across her face. Her expression never changed.

"I am sorry, Detective, I don't know who that is?" Maria ensured she had eye contact with Jason at all times when she lied.

"Dee Quaid, Jack Quaid's estranged wife? Or widower now, I would say."

"I am sorry, Detective, I do not know who you are talking about? I am sure I don't know a Jack or a Dee Quaid." Maria wasn't going to slip up. The more this line of questioning went on, the stronger Maria became. Jason was really out of cards. He thought about playing the code card and murderers, even asking her about the Real Avengers. He felt that Maria was strong but he couldn't tell that she had been lying. He had been bettered, it was as simple as that. A few moments had passed as he looked at his pad.

"So you don't know a Jack Quaid?"

"No, Detective, I don't know a Jack Quaid or a Dee Quaid. Should I?" Jason wasn't sure. He didn't know how this all knitted together. He had hoped the sound of the name would have sparked something. It didn't. Again there was silence, too much of it.

"Is there anything else I can help you with, Detective? I have quite a busy day ahead of me. You see, there is only me now. My mother has her charity work. But only me to look after the Mellor interests." Jason knew that was the brush-off. She had answered all the questions he dared ask. There was little else he could say.

"Not at this moment, Miss Mellor." Jason stood up, followed by Roberto and handed Maria his card.

"If you hear from your man or my sister, I would truly appreciate a call, Miss Mellor." Maria took the card.

"Of course I will, Detective. Immediately." Jason and Roberto left the boardroom. Maria sat back down and picked up her phone. She sent a text. All it said was "I will think about it x". He deserved a kiss after the pizza last night. That was all he was getting though, for now. As she placed her phone back on the desk, James entered the room.

"Is everything Okay, Maria?" James had stood outside the door for the whole meeting. He could hear every word that had been spoken.

"Yes, James, they are just looking for Alex. I nearly said aren't we all." James didn't respond. He didn't want her to question why they still hadn't caught up with them.

"The car is ready for the lake house."

"Good, let me get some things from the office as I am heading home after we have paid Mrs Quaid a visit." Maria left the boardroom, followed by James.

* * * *

Oliver wanted to get out of Colorado and into Kansas as soon as possible. If they were being followed, then Oliver knew Alex's DNA would have been all over John Andrews. Her knuckles showed that in the shower last night. Alex had been better but something was worrying her and Oliver. Her appetite for food was up, and so was her appetite for him. These were good signs. He detected a small dream last night, no sweats or calling out, but it wasn't completely restful as it had been before. They discussed it and Alex tried to brush it off.

Alex was worried. About the words from John Andrews, they had been ringing in her head. The escalation process, the need, the ongoing need. Yesterday had been good for her. She didn't feel bad about what she had done to him. Not after what he had done to all those kids but this morning, as she awoke, she could feel it. The craving was coming. Oliver could see it. It had been less than twenty-four hours this time. They both knew that wasn't a good sign.

* * * *

James pulled up outside the lake house. This was the part of the job that Maria didn't like. Her father once sat her down and gave her a speech on business. He had been a little drunk from

161

a charity function and Michael had been playing up a lot over the previous months. He was looking to her to take over from him in the future. He told her that she would have a responsibility to keep the family name clean. To ensure that the business didn't fail. It wasn't just a responsibility to the family. It was the world she would be looking after. Worldwide the Mellor groups with the oil, technology, research, hospitals, property. Millions of people relied on them every day for employment. The research was saving lives. The technology was shaping the future of the human race. She had never thought of it like that. She had never understood the pressure that the family were under to be leaders. To stay strong for all of those people was a great responsibility. The business had to succeed in any case. This speech, his speech always played in her head when she had to deal with something that questioned her morals. Kidnapping was one of those. They got out of the car. Dee was sitting at the dining room table. There were four guys in the room with Dee when they entered the house. As James and Maria did, the others left. Maria looked Dee directly in the eye. She could see the bruising and the cuts but tried to block them out. Dee winced at the sight of James. He had hurt her and she knew he wouldn't think twice about doing it again.

"Mrs Quaid. I am sorry for the delay in coming to meet you." Maria took a seat on the opposite side of the table and James stood behind her.

"Miss Mellor." Dee recognised her. Alex had spoken so much about them that she googled them to find out more. She had seen dozens of photos of her and her brother at major events around the world. She was prettier in real life.

Something Dee thought but this wasn't the time and place to bring this up.

"Good, we know each other, that is a good start. I understand that you have spoken with James and given him all the information that you have with regards to Alex and the situation we find ourselves in?" Dee just nodded. She wanted to say the words spoken and beaten, but again she knew this, wasn't the time. She had been kidnapped. By people she knew that bred murderers. She was going to be lucky to walk out of here with her limbs intact.

"So, Mrs Quaid, is there anything else that you can help us with? Anything you may have forgotten to tell us, anything you may have forgotten to tell James?" Dee looked at James. He had everything he had asked of her. Maria knew that. She was testing her, letting her know that James asked the questions and gave out the punishment should he not get the right answers.

"No, I answered everything you, he asked of me." Dee spoke softly.

"And you said you met with the president once, and not heard anything from her since? And it has been three months since you last spoke to Alex, which was just before my father's death?" Dee was trying not to look at Maria. She figured the best thing she could do was sound vulnerable and weak. It may have been the only way to save her life.

"Yes that is correct, Miss Mellor."

"Did you know her plan? Did you know she intended to kill my father?" Dee hadn't expected that question. She didn't know what to say. Alex had told her Christopher Mellor was a really powerful person. She never once said she would kill him though.

"I don't believe she intended to do that. Her plan, as far as I knew, was to get him to confess to everything that had been going on. She didn't give me all the details other than she was now going to be heading to Washington. Then she was going to give all the evidence to the president. And if something should happen to her, then I was to give the information I had to the president." Maria believed her, she sounded too genuine.

"James has updated me with what you told the president about. Can I ask you a point, Mrs Quaid? Do you believe that Alex told you everything?" Dee paused before answering as to compose herself on which side she was on.

"Honestly, no. I believe she only told me what she wanted the president to know. I was just a friend who would ensure the truth got out if something went wrong." As soon as those words were out of her mouth she wished she hadn't said them. She wanted to correct herself by saying she wouldn't say anything to anyone now. But it was too late, Maria was already standing.

"Thank you, Mrs Quaid. I am sure you understand the need for secrecy in these events, Mrs Quaid." Dee just nodded at Maria.

"Nothing that has happened should ever be repeated, Mrs Quaid. I want you to know James is only a few minutes away at all times. Should you remember anything." Dee knew that was a threat. One to tell her there was more pain or worse just a moment away at all times. She just nodded again.

"Then we have an understanding. My men will take you home." There was a sigh of relief from Dee. Maria stood and walked out into the hallway. James followed. She whispered in his ear and left the house. She went back to the car and James followed a few minutes later. Maria was already on her phone. Another three messages from the vice president. She had him hooked, she knew that. He had her hooked a little too, it was a match made by her mother. Maria was now convinced that she certainly was a good matchmaker.

"So we are heading home, Maria?" James sat in the driver's seat.

"Wait a moment, James." Maria sent a text back to Damion. He had asked her opinion on tie colour for the afternoon's meetings. She replied to his message choosing the blue one. It suited him. She took that as a good sign too. Asking her opinion twelve hours after the date. Showed that he was really keen. He valued her opinion.

Maria watched as the front door opened and they brought Dee out. Maria had wanted to see her leave. Everything she was doing from phone wires to kidnapping to Mr Quaid's death with a pillow, these were her protecting her family. Her fortune. Her employees. Her life.

Two men carried the body and they placed Dee in the back of the SUV in front of them. Dee was never going to be making her art class, ever again.

"Now it is time to go."

Chapter 8

It had been three days since they left Colorado. They had only managed to get to Dayton Indiana before Alex's demise was in full flow. She had shared her fears with Oliver as they left, about what John Andrews had said. Somehow that had stuck in her head and Oliver was sure it had increased the intensity of Alex's conditions. She had been susceptible to his influence. That was something he was going to have to watch out for in the future.

He couldn't risk taking her any further without a case. He knew it had to be something that would buy him a couple of days across country to get to Maria and the cure. It needed to be something bigger than The Cowboy. James had kept Oliver abreast of the situations regarding the cure. There was a meeting in town on Friday and the scientists would be bringing the cure with them. James had ensured they would be bringing enough for Alex. Maria had wanted to see it. She wanted to physically touch it as it could have saved her brother. Their trials had increased and all results so far had been positive. This gave Oliver a goal.

Oliver had checked them into a motel last night while Alex was still sleeping. Then he set up the laptop and the tracker and started his search. They would stay there until he had his Alex back, for a little time at least.

* * * *

"I know it is early, Dad, I can't sleep. I can't stop thinking about it. It's haunting me." Jason had explained to his father about the meeting with Maria as soon as he left her office. Maria had controlled the meeting from the start. He couldn't get a read on her. She was either really good at lying or she was telling the truth about not knowing what Alex was doing or where she was. She didn't know who Dee or Jack were, Maria had convinced him of that.

They walked out onto the porch so that Alex's mum didn't overhear the conversation. They sat on the chairs facing into the garden.

"Jason, you said you believed Maria Mellor. She didn't lie about the Institute or the fact that her father had been working with Alex. Something we thought, but we hadn't had confirmation of? That is something you should be taking out of your meeting. The real avenger's or whatever we are calling them, we are, what, ninety-nine per cent sure that is her now. That makes sense to us now. Given who they are dealing with. Is there a secret organisation taking out serial killers? It would seem so? I don't like it and we have to deal with her on her return, but we know she has professional help with her also. At least one other person that we know of? That also explains how they are surviving, if they had Christopher Mellor's money backing them. You said yourself that the Mellor security looked like ex forces. Maria said she had her father's best man with her. She is safer than we thought. She has money and resources. These are all things we know due to your meeting. You did a good job, Jason. Dee's disappearance doesn't have to be connected to the Mellors? Presuming she has definitely been kidnapped? She is tied up somewhere in this case with the president? If she knows something that could jeopardise national security, the secret service may have taken her. To God knows where." Fred's words were comforting Jason. Fred had been thinking them over for the last few days. Trying to make sense of what Alex was up to. He had his own thoughts that he wasn't ready to share with Jason as they were still sounding extreme in his head.

"Dad, I know. I have been playing the same thing over and over in my head. What I don't know is how we find Alex now? We have no leads and no one to talk to? I know Alex, she would contact us if she could. Why hasn't she? This secret mission doesn't sit well with me. It is too dangerous." They sat in their chairs. Jason automatically placed his hand to the right, feeling for the cooler. It was still nine a.m. There was no beer on the porch. Fred smiled at him. He knew what he had done. It had been such a frequent occurrence.

"I have registered her as a person of interest in the Craig Curle case. Just as a person we would like to talk to. That way she is on the list of every police force wanted list, in all states. If she is spotted, we will have her home. It is all we can do. I have told your mother also. It may hold her sane until we get Alex home." Jason knew it was the right thing to do. It was all they had left.

* * * *

Maria entered the kitchen. Carly was at the stove making pancakes. Saturday had come around again. There was juice poured and coffee brewed.

"Morning, dear." Carly poured the coffee as she walked in the door.

"Morning, Mum." Maria kissed her mother on the cheek and sat at the counter. The paper was there but she didn't pick it up. She could tell her mother was expecting her to, as she kept looking over her shoulder. Maria got back up and walked out of the kitchen. A few minutes later she returned with a stack of magazines and sat at the counter. They were both smiling to themselves as Maria sat down.

"So here is your first stack of pancakes, dear." Carly placed them on the plate in front of her. She then turned back to the stove. There were half a dozen pancakes on Maria's plate.

"What do you mean, first stack? Mum, I will be the size of a house if I eat all of these." Carly ignored her and continued to cook.

Maria tore at the pancakes while dipping them in syrup. She flicked through the magazines as she ate. Carly put another stack on the table and then went back to the stove. Maria was intrigued by her mother's actions. Six was normally enough for them both to share. There was a smile on Carly's face but she wasn't talking. She continued and made another batch, brought them to the table and then sat down.

"Finally finished then, Mum? Eighteen pancakes? Are you expecting anyone?" Maria looked directly at Carly, she was still smiling.

"No, dear, are you?" Carly then took a few pancakes and put them on her plate. Maria knew. She knew that her mother knew. She knew everything, that woman always knew everything. These pancakes were for a reason though. Maria decided not to play her game.

"No, not me." Maria went back to her magazines. They ate in silence for a while. Each waiting for the other to talk first.

"By the way, dear, you have missed wiping some of the eyeliner off." Maria reached for her eye.

"The left one, must have been on account of you rushing so much this morning. You know when you got home about an hour ago and ran up the stairs to get changed." Maria choked on her pancake.

"There are twenty bedrooms in this house and five between yours and mine. How the hell did you hear me come in?" Maria had taken her shoes off and carried them up the stairs as not to wake anyone. She thought she had got away with it.

"We don't use the word hell in the kitchen, my dear. I am your mother, I hear everything. It is my job." Maria laughed at that. It brought a smile to Carly's face also.

"So where did he take you, you know, on your second date?" Maria was aiming to put pancake in her mouth again but she thought better of it. It was going to be one of those conversations. One where her mother knew everything but she was going to pry more out of her.

"What? Wait, how did you know it was my second date?"

"As I said, I am your mother. I also know the pizza was good. I have had pizza from there, believe it or not. It was good when I had it too. That was a few years ago now though." This shocked Maria. She could never see her mother in a pizzeria. Cocktail dresses and summer balls were more of her type of evenings out.

"No, you have not. Mum, you don't eat pizza?"

"No, dear, your father didn't eat pizza. I did in my day. I love it. Even now, all the time we spent in Italy I used to sneak off for a slice. I am sure your father knew but he never mentioned in… I suppose I can just order one now. Had not really thought about that until just now. Maybe I will dial one for tea tonight." Carly was laughing to herself about the thought of that. Maria was shocked, she was realising how little she actually knew about her mother. She was always there to support her husband. Attended and planned the balls and the galas but never really in the limelight. Maria was beginning to realise there was a lot more to Carly Mellor than she knew.

"Dial a pizza, that is so funny, Mum. Okay, I have to ask, what is it with the pancakes? There is enough to feed an army here."

"Don't change the subject, dear, you were about to tell me where you went on your second date, and with regards to the pancakes, I just thought you might need the energy this morning. Given the time you got in." Maria knew exactly what that meant. She was fishing to see if she needed the energy after last night's activity. If she had been paying more attention to Maria eating rather than talking she would have realised that she had already eaten five pancakes. Maria had been trying hard to contain her happiness all morning. It had been so long since she'd had a connection with someone. Spent the night with someone. They hadn't slept. Damion had carried her to bed around midnight and they made love to the early hours. It was everything she had dreamed it to be. Afterwards they lay watching the sun come up and talking. Damion made coffee and toast for breakfast. Her mother was right though, she needed the energy now. Just to keep her eyes open. She had forced herself to stay awake to cover her tracks and failed.

"Mum." Carly just smiled. Maria's face was glowing. She didn't need to push it any further.

"We just stayed in and watched a movie. It had been a long day for the both of us. That is all you are getting out of me." Maria was back to her food.

"Where did you watch the movie?" Carly didn't need to push it any more but now this was for fun. She was teasing Maria now.

"At his house. We ordered in. He doesn't smoke. He has Captain America slippers that his niece bought him. He loves cold pizza. And he is a good kisser... No more, Mum. That is all you are getting out of me." There was silence as they both smiled at each other.

"That's nice... Just one more question, I promise. Will there be a third date, Alex?" Carly could tell by the look in her eyes, and the fact that Maria had received in the region of eleven texts since they sat for breakfast that there was going to be. Each time her phone bleeped she had picked it up and smiled.

"Yes, Mum, there will be a third date." Maria blushed as she said that.

"Good, then keep your strength up and eat some more pancakes." Carly pushed the sharing plate closer to her.

* * * *

Alex was still sleeping. Oliver had been over and over it again. There was only one case. One case in the area big enough to quench Alex's thirst. He didn't like it. It was not that the case wasn't justified. It was. Murder, violence, rape, prostitution and drugs, they had all been involved. Antoni Lannazzi, an Italian man in his early thirties. Oliver knew as soon as he saw the name it was only going to mean one thing. He was right, he did his research on the family. Cincinnati had been the base of their operations, but Antoni was so far up the food chain he never really went where all the action was. He had a bunch of legitimate businesses from Middletown to Sharonville, all money laundering operations. Antoni was a true Italian; his family traced all the way back in the old country. His father ran most of the USA underworld. His grandfather was still back in Italy but pulled his father's strings from there. Oliver sat and watched his movements over the days on the tracker. Nothing was ever the same. Apart from Sundays. Sundays he would go to church. It was only a small church off Walnut Street. Lunch he had presumed had been a family affair as it was at the same house every week also. Sunday night was a different matter. He would spend at least three hours every Sunday night in a warehouse to the west of the town. Oliver figured this was work. He couldn't think of another reason. If they were going to take care of him, it would have to be then. There was a good chance he wouldn't be alone, and a good chance it would be enough for Alex to quench her thirst. It meant another restless night in the motel though. Oliver closed down the laptop and headed out for supplies.

* * * *

"Do you know, Mum? A late lunch was a great idea. I don't think I have been to Dad's golf club since, well, you know." Carly did know. She had still been to the golf course once a week on ladies' day. She had learned to play golf for her husband and their business interests. Over the years she had learned to love it and developed a network of friends to play with.

"It was hardly a choice to have a late lunch, dear. You slept most of the day away." There was a smile across Carly's face as she said that. They both knew why Maria was tired. They were escorted into the dining room and shown to their table. It was overlooking the eighteenth green. It used to be the captain's table but after the Mellor Foundation brought the club they had made it their table. Water and wine appeared at the table. The Mellors had their own wine collection at the club and Carly had ordered ahead to ensure the quality. The white needed to be at the right temperature and the red needed to breathe.

"I know. Sorry, Mum. I was tired." Maria wasn't sorry. It was a good day. Damion had been very attentive this morning. It reassured Maria. After being out of the dating game so long, she had been worried that this was just a one-night thing. It wasn't, he was clearly interested in her more than that.

"So, dear, how is work? How is your father's empire? I guess, your empire now. I know he would be so proud to see you in that role. Anything exciting happened this week?" For a moment Maria stopped thinking about Damion and her mind switched to Dee. There had been no choice. Maria spent twenty-four hours running it through her head. Dee knew too much. The fact that she had told Jack's father was on her. She had been sworn to secrecy from everyone yet she still spoke to him. It was on Dee that he died. Maria had told James on exiting the lake house to make it quick. She didn't say anything else. The body wouldn't be found. Over the years, working for her father she knew that making bodies disappear had been a skill of her workforce. None had ever returned.

"It is fine, Mum. I can't really say it is mine. It is ours, at best. Still feels like Dads though. They are big shoes to fill. I am just trying to keep it going. I am learning a lot every day though. So who knows, over time?" The time she had spent with her mother since the death of her father told her that she was probably better equipped to run the business. She had started to see her mother in a different light now. There was a strength there she had never seen before. But they had the talk. Carly had asked Maria to step up. Not the same calibre talk her father had given her but very similar. Very much focused on understanding the importance of the work and the people that relied on them for their livelihoods.

"I think you are doing a remarkable job, Maria. I am so proud of you. Your father would have been too." Maria had the feeling that her mother was watching from afar. Ensuring she was doing well. She had influence that far outstretched even Maria's comprehension. It was comforting.

They reconfirmed their order to the waitress as she topped up the wine.

"This is a good wine choice, Mum." Maria was keen to get off the topic of work. This was her time with her mother. Her father had always told her to protect her mother from the dark side of the business. It was a necessary. But not something for her mother to know about.

"Thanks, it is not very often we get to share a bottle of wine, is it?" Maria knew this to be true. Neither of them really drank in the week. There had always been wine on the table but that had been for Christopher and Michael. Since they were gone they stopped serving it. Water was good for both of them.

"No, I guess not? We should do it more." Maria's phoned bleeped again. It hadn't stopped all day.

"Silent, dear, you know the rules of the club." As owners, they had to abide by the rules. It was an old traditional golf club. Phones were not allowed. It had only been the last ten years that they had invited women into the main dining hall. Maria picked her phone out of her bag and put it on silent. She read the latest text from Damion. She reread the message just to ensure she had read it correctly. Then instead of placing the phone in her bag, she placed it on the table. Their first course appeared in front of them. It was smoked salmon on a cracker with soft cheese. Almost the size of a silver dollar. They both looked at each other. Christopher would always moan about the size of the portions. They shared a laugh without saying a word.

Two bottles of wine and three courses later, Maria picked the phone back up. She had watched the phone keep lighting up over lunch but wanted to spend the time with her mother.

"I expected you to pick that up sooner. Must have flashed at least a dozen times. He certainly is keen on you, dear. Either that or this vice president job can't be that busy?" Carly was laughing as she spoke. The wine had gone to her head a little. They both were feeling the effects of the wine. It was a good feeling. They had laughed all afternoon. It had been refreshing for Maria to see her mum so happy after all the tragedy they had been through.

"Lunch with my mum comes first. Besides, I needed time to think. Isn't there a rule about drunk texting anyway?"

"We aren't drunk, my dear. Not yet anyway. What do you have to think about?" Maria scrolled through the texts to ensure that she showed her mother the right one. There was a few she didn't want her mother to read. She then handed her the phone. Carly read the text.

"Oh, and I guess you are feeling that was a surprising text? So early in whatever this is?" Carly was keen to avoid the word relationship. For fear of scaring Maria.

"It is, Mum, isn't it? We have just been on two dates. People don't do that after two dates, do they?" Carly smiled at her daughter.

"I think you would be amazed what people do after two dates." The pause from her mother was for the obvious reason. Maria knew it.

"Do you know, on our first date your father took me to L.A. to a film opening? Private jet. Well, his father's jet. He really pulled out all the stops. It worked. We, were inseparable from that point onwards. He was quite the charmer." Carly always smiled when talking of her late husband, forgetting his conduct in business. Carly loved him for who he was.

"But, Mum, I guess it would be normal if he were normal but he is the vice president. There will be press, lots of press. We would be almost announcing we are in a relationship to the world, wouldn't we?" Carly's intuition paid off. She knew the relationship word would scare her.

"So, do you like him, dear? You said yourself there would be a third date? Have you thought about a fourth, fifth? Holidays? If you have? Then is it worth the risk of a little press?" Maria did like him. A lot. The last week had her head in a spin about him. Even knowing everything else that had happened, he had been the thought above all others. She just smiled at her mother.

"Maria, you are quite the catch. You are stunningly beautiful. A successful businesswoman with a brilliant mother. Why wouldn't he be throwing everything he has at you? He must feel like he has won the lottery. If I were you, I would embrace this. I would go, my dear. You deserve a break. It will do you good." Maria never had the confidence of her brother. They were both talked about in the press about how beautiful they were and while Michael loved the attention, Maria was always happy to stay away from it.

"I am so glad you said that, Mother. She took the phone back and scrolled ahead a few messages and passed the phone back.

"Oh, now that is a surprising text." Her mother laughed again.

"Yes, if I am going, so are you, apparently a dozen people. Tuesday to Thursday." Carly took a sip of wine. She called the waiter over and ordered another bottle.

"Mum, we have had two bottles already."

"Let's celebrate, it will be fun. We could do with the break. Hopefully they have finished the new stables. I can teach you to play golf. It is only four holes but it is fun. A little bowling. Yes, it will be fun. It has been far too long since I have been to Camp David."

Chapter 9

"Dad, you didn't need to treat us all. I know that it is Tuesday, but I was so looking forward to a home-cooked meal… Really looking forward to one actually." She stopped to think about that for a second. The words home-cooked meal had meant so much to her. She had been wanting to say them for so long. She looked around the table, her mother, father, brother, sister-in-law and nephew all sitting at the table laughing and joking with each other. Although they were clearly in a restaurant, this felt like home to her.

"If I cannot treat my family, then who can?" Her father was happy. Not just happy, he was elated. She couldn't remember seeing him like that. She looked around the table again. The chair next to hers was empty. She was waiting for him. He was supposed to have been here by now? It was time for him to meet the family. A pair of hands covered her eyes. She could smell the aftershave as he leaned into her.

"Guess who?" She smiled. She knew who it was.

"Oliver." He leaned around and kissed her on the cheek. He then greeted each of the family in turn. They knew him. This wasn't the first time they had met. Her mother kissed him.

Her nephew hugged him. She was sure they hadn't met before. He sat down next to her and held her hand under the table.

"How is work?" She was shocked by the question.

"Mum, we don't discuss work at the dinner table" Her mother smiled at her.

"That is the dinner table at home. We can discuss anything you like here. We have no secrets." She was sure there were secrets. There were always secrets, things that couldn't be said. She wasn't allowed to tell them everything?

"No secrets, you hear that? Your mum says no secrets. Maybe we should tell them?" She smiled at him. She knew it was love. Deep down it had always been love. The look in his eyes told her that. He was smiling. Just like her father, not just happy, really happy. Yes, they should tell her family. It was huge news. It was life-changing news. They would be so happy for them.

"We are…" She stopped. Over his shoulder she could see them. Chris Masters and James Winters having dinner on the next table. Why weren't they with them? Why weren't they having dinner with them? She became fixated with them. She knew why they weren't sitting with them. She knew there was a reason. It was coming back to her. Blood started to trickle down the side of Chris Masters' head. That was the reason. The marketplace. The gun. He was…

"We are?" He pulled her back to the conversation. As he did, they changed. Chris and James were no longer there. There were just two random people having dinner. She stood up. She was sure they were there? They were just there?

"I swear…" He stood up next to her. He was always there.

"Are you okay, dear?" She shook her head. He whispered in her ear.

"It's okay, it can be our secret a little longer. We don't need to tell them tonight." They both sat back down. The first course came. She watched as plate by plate was laid to her family. Their food looked amazing, fish, vegetables, all very nouvelle cuisine. Hers was placed in front of her. Chicken balls and noodles. Chinese. It was a main. Everyone else had starters. Why was hers different? She needed to complain to the waitress. There had been a mistake. She looked up at her. It was Sophie. Sophie Simpson. She jumped back out of the chair. The chair fell backwards and so did she. Sophie. Sophie was there and she was pregnant. Still pregnant, the baby was still alive. It can't be, she knew it couldn't be. She knew Sophie and the baby had gone. Sophie and her baby were dead. Sophie was the first. She had to die. The baby had to die. The cocktail from the Brown Institute. That baby could not live. Not Paul and Sophie's baby.

He was there again. He picked her up. He was always picking her up. He had taken care of her. Sophie had gone. The waitress remained, but it wasn't Sophie.

"Sit back down. I think it was the pressure of, you know." She sat back at the table. Her family hadn't noticed. They weren't asking her what was going on? They were still having fun, smiling, eating, drinking. It was beautiful to watch, but something wasn't right here. They finished starters. Her food disappeared. Half a dozen waiters turned up around them. They were all holding plates with silver domes over the top. Her family gave a round of applause. The waiters bent down and placed the plates on the table. Alex could see them all. The waiters, her ex-partner and his brother Paul, and Mike Simpson. Her ex-colleagues Chris Master and James Winters were back. The late Dr Jonathan Smith from the Brown Institute was also there. There was one other, to her right, she could feel him there. She knew who it was. She didn't need to turn around. His scent was strong. As he leaned down to take the lid off the dome, she could see the reflection of his blue eyes in the silver.

"Do you have the rings?" Her head turned to Oliver standing next to her. In front of her was her captain. She looked around. She was in a church. She was in a church and dressed in white. This was her wedding day. Her wedding day. She began to smile. Her hand moved to her belly. It was big. She looked down. It was her wedding day and she was pregnant. She rubbed her belly. She looked around again. She could make out some of the people in the church. Her family were there, she could feel them.

"Do you have the rings?" She paid attention back to the captain. She smiled at him. Oliver spoke.

"The best man does." He turned and she could see out of the corner of her eye someone climbing the steps. The world turned to slow motion. She knew who was the best man. He had always been there. Since her and Oliver had been together he was with them. There had been three people in this relationship from the beginning. She knew who was bringing the rings.

They lowered the coffin into the ground. She stood and watched them. It was raining but she didn't care. Her heart was aching; she knew that she had loved him. They had loved him. Looking down at her right hand she could feel someone holding it. Her son. He must have been five, maybe six. He had lost his father and she had lost her husband. It was a military funeral. He had been a military man. A good man. Everything he had done had been for the right reasons. As the first shot fired, she felt his hand on her shoulder. He was always just behind her. Not knowing why, she put her hand on his. It had felt natural.

She sat at the table. The room was dark. A single spotlight shone on the table in front of her. On the table was a chessboard. Only a few pieces remained. She was white. He was black. She knew that had meaning. She just didn't know why. She couldn't see who she was playing but she knew who it was. It was him.

"It is your move." She recognised the voice. She knew it was her move. The game had been playing for a long time. Too long now. They both wanted it over.

"It's been a good game. But it is your move?" She sat looking at the pieces on the board. Counting them, there was only one move left.

"I know, and what of my son?" He was important to her. There was something telling her that he needed to be taken care of.

"He is a good man now, real chip off the old block?" She didn't like the sound of that. Why did he say that? Chip off the old block sounds like they are the same. Her son is the same as her.

"You are not with him, are you?" There was a silence.

"Before I make my move, tell me you are not with him." There was silence again. It was weighing on her.

"I am only with you, I have always only been with you, and I will be with you now." He leaned forward out of the darkness. She could see his eyes first as he came into the light. Those eyes had followed her through her life. He had followed her. He was always with her. He placed a gun on the table. She knew the move. She knew the time had come. He leaned back into the darkness. She picked the gun off the table. She knew her move, the only move left. She placed the gun under her chin and put her finger on the trigger.

"Wait!" he called out to her. He leaned forward again. They were looking each other directly in the eye.

"How Many?" Her heart sank at the words. The words had followed her entire life too. Ever since that day. That day walking into Jack Quaid's house. Since that day, those words were coming. She couldn't hear them at first. They started as a soft whisper. But they were coming. The Brown Institute, the Mellors, Michael, Maria, Oliver, they were all there. The words were weaving in and out of the people from her life. Her son flashed before her eyes. His smile. The park. His hair. His eyes. His eyes were somehow different, somehow bluer. Was her life flashing before her eyes? Was this what it felt like? Just before your case was solved.

"How many?" he asked again. She knew she had to answer the question. The question was out there to be answered. It was time. She never said the words out loud. She whispered them. It was how they started and it was how she wanted them to end.

"Too many." As the whisper left her lips, the trigger was pulled. She could feel the heat of the explosion under her chin, she could feel the bullet as it travelled through the gun and out of the barrel. It pierced the skin, it started to travel up, through the bottom of her mouth. Her mind went back to the park, back to her son. He was laughing, spinning in the sunshine. His eyes. His eyes were blue, bluer than before. His eyes were, his eyes were, his eyes. They were Michael's eyes.

"No!" Alex screamed herself awake. Her first reaction had been to grab at her chin. To stop the bullet. She soon realised there wasn't one. It was all she realised, she had no idea where she was. Oliver was next to her. As with the dream, he was always there. Taking care of her. They were already parked just down the road from the Antoni Lannazzi warehouse.

"Alex, Alex, it's fine, it's me. Don't worry, I am here. We are here, the case, Antoni. It is time."

* * * *

"What do you pack for Camp David, Mum?" Maria and Carly were in Maria's wardrobe. It had been a twenty-one-bedroom house when they moved in. Maria's wardrobe had moved into its own room. Carly was helping her with her packing.

"You pack for everything, dear, riding, swimming, golf, the gym and dinner. Formal and informal. You don't always get to do everything, but a future first lady has to be prepared." Maria was looking at her mother.

"Stop teasing me, and don't tell me you have packed already? Maybe you should have been the first lady." Maria could really see her mother in that role. There was that strong silence about her. She could deal with anything.

"Yes, dear, I have packed. Not my first trip. Your father and I thought about running for office quite a few times. In fact, it was your father that was against it. We never really discussed why. He just said that he didn't want the world looking at him and our family." Maria was still staring at her mother. She was remarkable. She knew why her father would think about the presidency twice. Michael. Anyone digging into their family would find Michael. Her father would have been protecting him.

"Mum, I am still not sure about this. It is a big step." Carly walked over to her daughter and hugged her. She gave her a kiss.

"Maria. You have made some big steps over the last three months. This is just another one of them. I am so proud of you. This is a new beginning for you. This is a new beginning for us. We can face anything together. Trust me, this will be fun." Maria smiled. She knew she liked Damion, it was a big step for the both of them. Her mother had been so supportive about that. They were the words she wanted to hear. She always had the words she wanted to hear. She was confident that with her mother by her side she could achieve anything.

"I don't know how you do it but you always know what to say. Thanks, Mum." Carly returned to the packing.

"Lingerie, dear, do you have the right attire?" The words just rolled out of Carly's mouth as if they had meant nothing.

"Mum!"

* * * *

Oliver sat watching her as she was deep in thought. He knew this was getting worse. She had been lost to him again for a while.

"I have counted at least a dozen people in there, Alex. I need to know you are okay before we go in. There may be more. This is risky. I mean, real risky. These are professional men." Alex had been coming round for twenty minutes. It was so real, all of it. For the first time it hadn't just been about Michael and her. They were all there. She had a life. A life she dreamed of but it wasn't Michael-free. It was never going to be Michael-free until the end. Is that what the dream had been telling her? Had it been telling her, her only way out? No! She knew Michael meant the hunger. The hunger for the kill. She would never lose it. It was always next to her. She was going to be able to deal with that. Besides, they were heading for the cure. She wanted the cure. She wanted rid of Michael, didn't she? Didn't she? What was the gesture with the hand on the shoulder? If Oliver wasn't here, would she really be looking to Michael for comfort? Thoughts were twisting in her mind now. Was it Oliver that was between her and Michael or Michael that was between her and Oliver?

"I am good, Oliver. It was just a dream." She knew those words meant nothing. They meant nothing to her as much as they had meant nothing to Oliver. Nothing was just a dream any more. She hadn't told him the dream. It was too close to reality. Michael had been there. There with all of them. Her family, her friends. In broad daylight.

"It is always risky, Oliver. That is what we do. Antoni deserves to die." Oliver had never heard her say that before. It had always been about solving a case. She never used the kill or die word on purpose; it kept her in reality.

"Let's give it another ten minutes then go." Alex nodded to him. This worried him even more as she was happy to wait. There was still something in the back of his mind saying this was the wrong idea. They sat watching the clock as it ticked in the car. Exactly ten minutes later Alex stepped out of the car, followed by Oliver. They moved around to the back of the car. They suited up. With an unknown number of people inside, they needed vests. Alex had told them all too often when she was good that they needed them. In the heat of battle, she never remembered. She always did again afterwards, when she had had her fix. Paul Simpson would come flooding back to her. Screaming that she should wear a vest. Just as she had that day in the Marriot where he lost his life.

They needed a lot of weapons. Oliver had his fair share. He kept a full arsenal in the trunk of the car. Oliver was worried about her. He made sure they were fully packed before he closed the boot.

"Are we good, Alex?" She gave him a nod. She looked focused. That was the Alex they needed.

* * * *

"Dad, I have requested a week off. The sergeant has signed it off." Sunday dinner was over and they were back on the porch. Angela, Fred's wife, had thought about breaking the rule lately. Jason and Fred spent nearly every evening on the porch. Which wasn't healthy for either of their relationships.

"Don't go looking for her, Jason. Not on your own." Jason didn't respond.

"You know it is too dangerous." They both knew it was too dangerous.

"I know, Dad. I did think about tracing the Real Avengers. But if the task force attached can't find them, Then I am sure I won't." Jason sounded dejected at that thought.

"I am actually going to read Jack Quaid's novel, book, whatever you want to call it. I have been thinking about it, and I think that is what my sister has done. I know her, Dad. She was alone. She was looking for something to believe in since Paul had died. She has got into this guy's head and uncovered whatever he has uncovered. I am not sure what codes have to do with things. I think the answers are going to be in there." Fred knew it was going to be useless to argue with him. Jason was desperate now to find his sister.

"I think it could be a good idea, Jason." Fred wasn't sure. But if it gave his son peace then that was good enough for him at the moment.

* * * *

Oliver had watched the comings and goings of the warehouse as Alex slept. He knew there were a dozen at least in there. They all looked armed. It was the reason he ensured they were wearing vests. There was no plan other than the fix for Alex. Oliver knew this was dangerous. This was the Mafia they were taking on. If they got this wrong, there would be repercussion's.

"Follow my lead." Oliver set off in the direction of the warehouse. Alex followed behind. The plan, as much as they had discussed, was to gain entrance. They knew that there would be armed guards and they were never going to get past the pat-down. Oliver made his way to the door. As he knocked it was opened by an armed guard. Oliver could see directly into the warehouse. There were at least two dozen people in there. He could see guns, money and drugs. Antoni and his crew spent every Sunday night going through the week's accomplishments. This was their base of operations and not somewhere they needed to be. This was a mistake. There were too many of them. Oliver knew they needed to walk away. He looked at the guard. The words sorry, I have the wrong place were seconds from coming out of his mouth when he heard the first shot. Alex had shot the guard directly in the head. As she did, she walked past Oliver. Oliver had flinched as the bullet hit the guard straight between the eyes. The blood splattered back on him. He could see Alex entering the warehouse all guns blazing.

"Alex." It was too late, she was never going to hear him. He had to follow. Oliver started firing as he entered the building. They had the element of surprise. This helped with the first four to five people. After that it was a full-on gun battle. Oliver and Alex had been fortunate that the warehouse was full. Cars and crates everywhere. Good hiding places to shoot from. Alex had gone left and Oliver had tried to follow, but the gunfire had been too great. Oliver was taking out as many as he could. They weren't prepared for this. They were armed but they needed grenades, explosions, men. They needed more men than just the two of them.

"Alex, there are too many. We shouldn't have come in." Oliver was shouting across to her. She could hear him. He knew it. Her focus was on the people in front of her. Unbeknown to them, Antoni had already left the building through the back door. He was to be protected above everything else. His whole life, Antoni and his family had to deal with rival gangs trying to take over their territory. Their crews were expendable but they weren't. Alex and Oliver continued the shoot-out.

"Alex." There was no answer. Oliver knew he needed to get next to her.

"Alex, cover me, I am coming over." Alex heard that as she turned to face him. He mouthed counting to three and then she stood and fired. He ran across. A foot from reaching her, a bullet hit him just below the knee. He buckled and fell behind Alex.

"I am shot. Alex, I am shot." Alex turned. She could see he was down. The bullet had passed straight through his leg. Alex turned and carried on firing. She knew the situation was getting worse. She counted at least a dozen people still left. They had been working on getting closer to them. They didn't have long before they would be on top of them.

"Can you stand?" Oliver made it to his feet. He couldn't stand on it but he could lean against the wall and shoot. He counted the guns also. They were going to be no match for this.

"Alex, you need to go. We are not going to get through this." Alex could hear him. She knew he was speaking the truth. But there was no way to get out of this. They had come too far into the warehouse for Oliver to get back.

"We can't go back." This wasn't a question for Alex. She knew it was too far.

"We can't. But you can, I will cover you." Alex turned towards him.

"I am not leaving you here?" Alex couldn't believe he suggested it.

"Alex, there is no choice? I can hold them off while you get out through the door." The firing was getting more intense. The more that they spoke, the less firing they were doing and the closer Antoni's men were getting.

"No, if this is it, then this is it." Alex turned and continued shooting. She took another of Antoni's men out. Oliver grabbed her arm and forced his phone in her hand.

"No, Alex. It is not. Go get James. He will come and help. Think about it. They are not going to kill me. Antoni is going to believe that this is a hit. He is going to torture me until I give up who is behind this. Once you are out of here, I will surrender to them. It is the only way out of this." Alex was firing with one hand and listening to him at the same time. She knew he was right. Even through her rage she knew it was the only hope they both had of surviving and she wanted Oliver to survive.

"Alex, listen to me. I love you. I want to spend the rest of my life with you. But we aren't going to have any of that unless we get out of here. You get out of here and bring us some help. Get James. He will know how to take care of this. He is an expert." Alex shot five bullets in quick succession. She turned and kissed him.

"I love you too." They stopped and looked at each other for that was in reality a few seconds, but felt like a lifetime.

Without saying another word Oliver leaned against the crates and fired everything he had. Alex ran for the door. As she got to it, she shouted back.

"We are coming back." Everyone heard it. That was the point. Alex had hoped that by saying that, it would help Oliver stay alive long enough to get help. Alex ran out of the building and down the road towards the car. By the time she reached it, she turned around, nobody was following. Oliver still had them pinned in. Alex sat in the car. She didn't want to leave him in there. She thought about driving the car directly into the warehouse to get him. But she knew that was just going to end both of their lives. Oliver had been right. The only way they were going to be able to get free of this was with James' support. Alex drove. There were tears rolling down her face as she did. The rush of the attack had her focusing more. It also had her closer to reality again. She knew she was leaving the love of her life behind her as she fled. Somewhere where she may never see him again.

* * * *

"Miss Mellor, can I have a word?" Maria was sitting at her desk at home. Her plan had been to work from there today as her mother was home all day too. She was still nervous about the trip tomorrow. She could think of little else. So concentration was going to be a problem for her.

"Miss Mellor? It must be serious, James, as there is only me here? Come in." James entered the room.

"Sorry, I meant to say Maria. But it felt like a Miss Mellor moment." James looked uncomfortable. Maria could tell. Whatever he was about to say was important.

"What is it?"

"I think we have them, Maria. Oliver and Alex. They are close." There was a huge smile that came across Maria's face.

"Jesus, James, you had me really worried for a moment then. That's great news, James. How close are they?"

"Close enough that I think I should go and collect them personally." James knew as soon as the words left his lips he was playing all his cards. He knew that he would need to return with something or else he would be taken away from this. He had stalled on finding them for too long. It had been worrying him over the last few hours. The fact that it had been Alex phoning to explain everything hadn't helped. He didn't trust her.

"I can be there and back in a couple of days. I should probably take a couple of guys with me to ensure there is no trouble?"

"James, just deal with it and come back. It is still our top priority. I will be with the secret service until Thursday night. I will be safe. We can meet back here Friday morning for the meeting with the scientists. Take as many people as you need." James knew there were only a couple he could trust. Peter and Adrian. Both recruited by Oliver and both had loyalty to them both.

"Two will be fine, Maria. I understand that Oliver is injured which will make it a lot easier for us." Maria almost smiled at that point. She refrained from doing so out of respect for James. knowing they had been close. She trusted that

James was a company man, and would do what needed to be done.

"Okay, James. I need this to go away this week. You know what I mean by go away, don't you?" James knew what she meant.

"It will be taken care of, Maria." James left the room. Maria sat back in her chair. It had been a great start to what she expected to be an amazing week ahead. With Alex and Oliver out of the picture she knew that nothing would be able to stop her controlling the board and the direction of the business.

Chapter 10

Alex had barely slept. She had phoned James as soon as she returned to the motel. She lay cuddled up on the bed. Crying at the fact that she had left Oliver in there. Crying at the thought that she had started the killing. She could hear Oliver's words over and over again in her head saying that they shouldn't have gone in. It was too much. Her passion had taken over her. It was John Andrews. His words were coming true. As the door opened she saw the gun at the guard's side and her gun was out in front of her. She shot without thinking. As if it were natural. The urge was too strong to stop herself. This made her cry even more. Had she finally lost control of herself? She was begging for the release. The release from Michael and from her dreams. As she lay there, she knew that the feeling wasn't the same. Killing from a distance. Killing in a shoot-out. It didn't cure her hunger like the others. Not like standing one on one with someone. It almost felt like she had been in a video game. Or at a fair shooting at toy ducks. They fell over but it didn't mean anything. If she didn't see the kill, it didn't count.

The TV was on in the room. Alex kept it on. She didn't want to sleep. She knew he was there, there in her sleep. Ready to completely take over her. She needed Oliver close. She knew that he kept watch over her. Nothing could hurt her if he was there. All she could see now was him leaning against that crate, firing. A glimpse as she shouted out when she ran away from the fight. The fight that she had caused. She knew that could have been the last time she saw Oliver. He could be dead. If he wasn't dead, he was certainly in pain, hurting given the company he was in. They were torturing him, she knew it. Somebody knocked at the door. She went to the window and checked. Before she saw the face, she saw the SUV and the black suits. She knew it was James. She grabbed her gun before opening the door. Oliver trusted him. But Alex didn't. Alex was convinced that James had killed Chris Masters in the marketplace. And then James Winters in his car. She knew he was following her from Grayling. He had already knocked her out once in the park, when she was dealing with Stephen Henderson. It was fair to say they had a past of violence between them. The fact that she shot him in the leg was the only comfort she had, that she had at least got one back on him. She opened the door.

"Alex, nice to finally catch up with you. Put the gun down, Alex. I am here to help you." Alex didn't listen, she just backed up to the bed. Keeping the gun out in front of her.

"I think I will keep it close to me, James." James closed the door behind him. Peter and Adrian remained outside.

"Alex, if we had wanted to take you out, we would have done it ages ago. Oliver is my friend. And I owe him my life. So whatever this is, this quest you are on, as long as he is with you, then so am I." Alex knew exactly what that had meant. If something had happened to Oliver and he was already dead, then James wasn't going to think twice about taking care of Alex. Alex relaxed her arm. She didn't drop the gun. It was still in her hand. She believed he was here to help.

"It would seem you have taken a step too far with this one then? Tell me everything. Don't leave out any details, Alex." Alex sat on the bed but kept her gun close as she told him the whole story. She kept the part about the dreams to herself. Just the facts with regards to the last couple of cases and what had led them to Antoni. James hadn't been really interested in the history. He could tell Alex was unstable. She had been rambling her way through the story to the events of last night. He put it down to the trauma of losing Oliver.

"What about the tracker?" Alex got up off the bed and opened the tracker. Antoni was at the warehouse. Oliver had been correct in his assumptions: they were not going to kill him straight off. They needed to know who ordered the hit. Antoni had been informed that they had him an hour after Alex had left the warehouse. He wanted to ask the questions personally. Antoni had appointments scheduled all morning. Knowing that they had Oliver strung up in the warehouse was exciting to Antoni, and making him wait was half of the fun. Antoni had only been asking questions for an hour. Oliver had given them nothing so far. This wasn't the first time he had been in this situation. He knew how to take pain. This was thrilling for Antoni. Most people would have cracked by now. Oliver was fast realising whatever they had done to Oliver in the Brown Institute had given him a taste for torture.

"If that is it, Alex, I suggest we get a move on then." Alex closed down the tracker. She was still dressed. She grabbed her vest off the floor and followed James out of the door. Thirty minutes later they were at the warehouse. It was beginning to get dark. They knew they didn't really have the time to wait for it to be pitch black. James drove around the premises. He could see two entrances and they needed them both covered. Peter and Adrian took the back as he and Alex took the front. Alex looked to James as they got to the door. She was expecting a "stand behind me" or a "stick close to me." She was going to get neither. James was only there for Oliver. James took out a walkie-talkie and just said "now". Peter and Adrian had set a charge at the back door. The explosion was one big enough to take the door and half a wall out. A minute later James kicked the front door in. It had worked. The charge at the back had drawn everyone in that direction. They needed to get to Oliver quickly. James went first. It wasn't hard to see Oliver. As soon as they entered the warehouse, they could see him strung up by the hands in the middle of the room. Antoni had liked an audience. He liked to ensure that his staff knew what would happen to them if they crossed him. James was firing and taking out Antoni's men. Each shot was a kill shot. Alex was following behind, hitting as many as she could. There was a second explosion. James didn't jump. He had been expecting it. Alex jumped. She didn't know the plan. They hadn't shared it with her. The only reason she was there was to save time. If Oliver was dead on arrival. Alex would be joining him in the same location. All Antoni's men were on edge. Especially when the third charge went off. None knew where to look for the attackers. Peter and

Adrian had been busy. By the time they joined the fight there were only three men left, surrounding Antoni in the middle of the warehouse next to Oliver. Antoni had a knife held to Oliver's side. Oliver had seen better days. There were cut marks and bruises everywhere but he was alive. Antoni had been having fun in his chosen career this afternoon.

"One more step and I will kill him." James looked directly at Antoni. He raised his gun and took out all three remaining guards in a matter of seconds. It happened so fast. Antoni didn't move.

"What, what the fuck do you guys want? Who are you working with? Whoever it is, I can pay you more. You can work for me and I will pay you triple what you are being paid at the moment?" Alex could hear the pleading in his voice. It had become a familiar sound for someone to plead for their life and too for them to try and buy their way out of the situation.

"Step away from Oliver, sir. We are only here for him. Nobody else needs to die." Antoni moved closer to Oliver. Trying to shield himself from all three angles. These were professional men. They had positioned themselves so there was nowhere to hide.

"Sir, I won't be asking you again. Stand away from Oliver and I will let you live." Alex was looking at James now. There was no way she was going to let him walk out of here.

"Sir, you have my word. Drop the knife and step away." Antoni looked around again. There was nowhere to go. He didn't really have a choice. Four armed people were bearing down on him and all he had was a knife. He dropped it and stood away from the body. Alex lifted her gun a little higher to take aim. As she did, she felt the hit. She knew what was coming next. The darkness.

When she came round, she was back in the motel. Her head was killing her. On the bed next to her was Oliver. She immediately reached out and hugged him. He moaned in pain. Oliver was still pretty out of it and James had given him a serious injection of painkillers to help with the pain.

"Sorry, I am sorry." She looked down. He had been completely patched up. James had seen to that. There were stitches and bandages. Antoni had spent nearly two hours torturing him. It had only taken James thirty minutes to patch him back up. There had been nothing serious. He had been prolonging the agony as he was having too much fun.

"He is going to be fine. There was nothing serious. Although I expect he will be in pain for a few days." Alex turned and James was sitting in the chair. He was drinking a beer and watching the TV.

"How long was I out for? This time." James could sense the emphasis on "this time" in her voice. Last time she had been out a good six hours after James had hit her.

"About four hours, I would say, Alex." He had a smug look on his face. He enjoyed knocking Alex out. She had divided the team he worked with. Oliver had fallen for her so much, he had left everything behind him.

"Losing your touch, James." He didn't respond to her. He knew it was bait for an argument.

"What of Antoni?" Alex was keen to know how they dealt with him.

"He is fine. We let him go." Alex could feel the rage explode in her.

"You let him go? He wasn't yours to let go. He was mine. You know what he is, you know what they all are? Look at what he did to Oliver?" The louder Alex got, the bigger James' smile became.

"What you all are, Alex. You don't get to play judge and jury any more. Whatever this was? This is over. We are heading back as soon as Oliver is fit enough to travel." Alex waited a minute and then went for her gun.

"It is not there, Alex. You don't think I am stupid enough to leave you a gun now, do you?" Alex checked her belt. The gun was gone. She went to her leg.

"Got that one too, just relax, Alex. I have sent the guys for some food. We can all crash here for a while. The cure is heading back home too. The plan is to intercept it at the hotel on the Thursday. I have ensured they bring enough for you, Alex. Then you, you and Oliver, you are going to disappear. For good, Alex. I don't care where in the world you go. But just go. And don't return. Then me and Oliver, we are even." There was a tone in James' voice that told Alex he meant every word of that. Alex didn't like being told what to do. She didn't like orders. She could feel the blood surging through her veins. |She hadn't had her fix. The whole events of the last twenty-four hours hadn't given her the fix she needed. Here she was, at least seventy hours until the cure and she could feel the desire already. With no Oliver to look after her, it was going to be a hard few days ahead. The dreams were going to be strong, there was little chance for sleep. Reality and her dreams were crossing over now. Alex knew he was coming.

* * * *

"The helicopters here, darling" Carly walked into Alex's office. She was already at the window watching it land.

"Who sends a military helicopter to pick up his girlfriend on a date, Mum? I am still not sure. This is a huge step." Carly walked up behind her and cuddled her from behind.

"Vice presidents, I guess. It is going to be fun Maria. A few days away will do us both some good." She watched as her men ran to the helicopter and loaded their luggage onto it.

Maria didn't move. A few minutes later the blades stopped turning. Damion stood out of the helicopter and walked towards the house. Maria went and sat in her chair as Carly remained at the window. When Damion arrived at the house he was shown to her office.

"Miss Mellor, your ride awaits?" Maria was at the desk looking at paperwork. She wasn't reading it. She just didn't want to seem too eager to jump on the helicopter with him.

"Thank you, Mr Vice President, we will be there directly." Maria nodded at him and then looked back down at the paperwork. He laughed and walked back out of the office and back onto the helicopter.

"That is so funny. Your father taught you well, Maria." Carly was laughing to herself as Damion left.

"No, Mum, that was all you, all you." Maria grabbed her handbag and she and Carly followed Damion.

* * * *

"You're early." Fred answered the door to Jason, Sandra and Ethan.

"I know, Dad. The joys of having the week off. You didn't think that we would miss Tuesday night dinner though, did you?" They went through to the kitchen.

"Your mum will be home shortly. She is at the market getting more veg." There was a laugh from Sandra as if to say three types are not enough.

"That's cool, grandad." Ethan went over and opened one of the drawers. He pulled out the colouring books and crayons and placed them at the table. Sandra sat next to him and they started to colour.

"Go on, Jason, on to the porch. Whatever it is, it has been eating at you for the last three hours and I guess that is why we didn't shower before coming over here?" Jason looked at Sandra and mouthed the word "sorry". He had almost forced her out the door when she returned from work. He didn't want to ring his father. What he had to tell him was in person.

The both went out onto the porch. Fred leaned down and pulled them both a beer.

"So, what is it that is so important that you have pissed off Sandra? Jason?" He could tell by the look on his face he was about to explode.

"It was in his book, Dad. Well, a file. Well, a file on them. And then if you read the book, his thoughts, I think, it all ties together. I think I know what is going on. All of it." Jason was struggling with his words. Not only with excitement but he was scared, scared that blurting something out something in clarity was going to get them into trouble. He thought again before saying anything else.

"Let's go out the back gate, Dad. Let's walk down the alleys. It is a lovely evening for a walk." Fred followed his son out of the back gate and down through the alleyways between houses. They led down to a small river which they knew no one ever walked down.

"I am scared, Dad, scared that someone will hear us."

"I think that we can talk here, Jason."

"Okay, but let's keep it down. I don't want anything to happen." Fred nodded at his son.

"Start from the beginning, Jason, and slowly."

"I found some files. In all those boxes. Alex must have left them there. I don't know if on purpose or not, Dad. But they aren't logged on any report. Anyway there are files on Michael and Maria Mellor. Quite a few other people also. They look like doctor's reports. Reports on their growth as kids." Alex had left them there. Not on purpose, she hadn't even thought about the files once she had the hard drive. Jack had only stolen a handful of hard copies. Now she had the whole database.

"So what does that have to do with the case?"

"So got me to thinking why would Jack Quaid have these? These look like originals, Dad. I have been digging. There was a burglary in the Brown Institute. Get this, when it was in Paris. It moved to Germany shortly after. I have checked flight manifests. Jack Quaid was in Paris, Dad. I think that he stole the files. That's not the thing though, Dad. The thing is his log. His book whatever it is, it mentions them. Jack went there. He went to their club and met with both of them? Michael and Maria Mellor."

"Okay, so he met with Michael and Maria. How does that help us?" Fred hadn't got up to speed with Jason. Somewhat due to his frantic speaking and the fact that he hadn't told him anything that was going to help them.

"No, Dad, he mentions a code. He mentions he knows what they are. He says he knew that Michael was a killer? Okay, he doesn't say that specifically but he indicates it. He said it was the code. Dad, I think that's what this is? I think it's something to do with killers. I think that is what we are missing. I know it sounds really mad, Dad, but I think the Mellors have been making killers. I think Michael was one of them." Fred was looking over his shoulder as he walked. That was a big statement to make. He didn't like accusing the Mellors of anything. He had been doing his own research into them and they were into everything and knew everyone. They were very dangerous people to be around.

"Calm down, Jason. I think you are getting a little over excited. If they were creating killers, before we get to the how and why they would do that, Jason, why would they make Michael one? It is not something that you do to family, is it? Christopher Mellor is hardly going to allow anyone to make his son a killer, is he? There is no need. They are billionaires." Jason knew that question would come at some point. He hadn't figured that out himself yet.

"I don't know, Dad. We have to work that out. But this is what it is. It fits. The code. They did something to him. Not just him. I think that is what this is all about. Think about it. Alex discovers it. She chases Michael down. That Deacon James case. Biggest serial killer of our time and Alex just happens to bump into him. Alex going for a three-hour drive, directly to that bar. That is not Alex? The Real Avengers, they are taking down killers everywhere. Some we didn't even know about. Hell, Vicars? Cults? And within days, Dad. Think about it, when they started there were two, sometimes three, a week. Nobody else knew where they were or who they were and now Alex can find a killer overnight? Somehow she knows about them. She is clearing somebody's mess up, I am sure of it. For who, is the question? The president? The Mellors? How far does this go?" Fred took a minute to take it all in. Jason was onto something. But that was a lot of information and a lot of unanswered questions to take in in one go. It did make sense once you got past the fact that someone could create a killer. Fred let it sink in before responding.

"Let's say all of that is correct. And, Jason, that is a big ask. Where do we take it from there? We are hardly going to the president of the United States? Or the secret service? And ask them if they are involved in creating and executing murderers with a secret task force headed up by your sister? You said yourself Maria Mellor ran rings around you? We don't know where Alex is so we can't get to her to collaborate with the story?" Jason had already been working on this.

"Yes, Dad, I know but she lied to us, Dad. We have just cause to bring Maria Mellor in. She told me she never knew a Jack Quaid or a Dee Quaid. That is clearly a lie as she knew Jack. He said he met her. I have it in writing."

Fred smiled at him. He knew that he wasn't going to give up on this. He was a good detective. He also knew they were playing well above their position as police officers here. They needed to be careful.

"It is a start, Jason. Then let's bring her in for a friendly chat, Jason. I reiterate that. A friendly chat. I will observe from outside." Jason's face was smiling. He had been hoping his father would agree with what he was doing.

"We will, Dad, but it won't be tomorrow. I spoke to her office just before Sandra got home. I knew you would agree with me and I wanted to know where to find her, should we want to talk to her again this week. You are never going to believe where she is, Dad? Camp David. She is not back to work until Friday. We can hardly follow her there?" Jason's smile disappeared.

"No, we can't. Jason, we keep this between ourselves. Don't talk about it or even mumble about it. Especially on the phone. These are clearly dangerous people." Fred was keen that Jason knew how serious this was. People were dying and missing and there seemed to be little evidence on either.

"I agree, Dad. We just have to wait till Friday, Dad. But we have her. I knew she was keeping something from me. Deep down I knew it. We have something on Maria Mellor that will take us a step forward." Jason had been feeling gutted following the death of Mr Quaid and Dee's disappearance. Now he had a real reason to be hopeful.

Chapter 11

Maria sat between her mother and Damion at dinner. She looked around the table at the guests. The president and her husband and their daughter Lisa. David and Denise Moore. They were both close friends of the president. He was heavily into food manufacturing and farms across the USA. During her campaign he had been the president's second largest sponsor next to the Mellors. All of his money was inherited from his father. He had in truth lost money since he took charge. Millions. It was common knowledge. Damion's uncle and aunty were there too. His mother and father had been invited also but his father had a business meeting in Italy which had meant that they needed to be out of the country Wednesday evening. There were just ten for dinner.

They had arrived yesterday morning and all the time they were there Maria could sense that the president had wanted to speak to her. She was nervous that was the whole, and only reason she was there. She started to doubt Damion and whether or not he was in on it. To get close to her to understand more about her father's work. She didn't want to disbelieve his real intentions. As he had been so affectionate over the last twenty-four hours.

When they arrived he gave her the option of staying with him or her mother. She stayed with him. It was really the reason she came. Her mother had been right as always. It was an amazing place to stay. They had played golf this morning, they had been kind to Maria, as she had only played a handful of times before, by giving her an eight-shot lead across the four holes. It had made no difference. She almost used them all up on the first hole. They lunched around the pool. Damion cooked on the barbecue and then they swam most of the afternoon. Tonight it was an early dinner and then they were to have a bowling competition. All the way through dinner they shared idol chit-chat. Maria could tell from the conversation that the president was going to make her move tonight. Every conversation she had, she included Maria into it. As if they were long-lost friends. She was sure everyone else was picking up on it. She wasn't disappointed. As they rose after dinner Victoria made a beeline for her before they left the dining room.

"Maria, can I have a quick word? It's about the Foundation. There is no need to wait for us. We will be right behind you." Carly and Damion looked at Maria. She nodded her head to both of them. They all left for the bowling. The president escorted Maria to a side room. She nodded at her guards and they left them alone in the room.

"Sit down, Maria. How about another brandy? I must say that I have a weakness for it while I am up here. It is the only place that you can really relax." Maria sat down in one of the leather chairs.

"Thanks, Victoria." Victoria poured the drinks and sat in the armchair opposite Maria. Maria suddenly had a moment of realisation of where she was. These leather back chairs felt like a brandy or whisky cigar room. Where presidents had relaxed for centuries. She started to think about the world-changing decisions that were made in these chairs. Then she realised she could be about to have one of them herself.

"Dinner was lovely, Victoria." Maria was keen to continue the idol chit-chat. She knew that wasn't what she was there for but she wasn't going to give up information easily.

"It was. Harry is an amazing cook. Been here for nearly ten years." The president took a sip of her drink while looking at Maria.

Maria knew this was going to be a game of chess. The more she got to know her, the more she understood the way Victoria worked.

"So, what would you like to discuss?" The president took another sip of her drink and then stood up. She walked over to the drinks cabinet and took out a file. It was at least three inches thick. She walked over and placed it on the table in front of Maria. Then sat back in the chair. She didn't say anything. She took another swig of her brandy. The silence continued. Maria knew she was being tested. She was strong enough to resist the urge to ask what it was. She waited her out.

"I would like you to read through that at your leisure, Maria." The president moved the file closer to Maria.

"Thank you, Victoria. I will. You are right, this is very good brandy." Maria resisted the urge to pick it up. She was also keen that the president knew she wasn't worried about what the file contained.

"Once you have, Maria, we can set up a meeting in the Whitehouse to discuss… the board, the Institutes and what we are going to do about them all. All eleven. Even though we only house two of them in my country. Given the fact they are all run from my country, I think I deserve answers on all of them." Maria took a sip of her drink. The president knew. She didn't need to look into the file. She knew from the look on her face. The fact that she said the board. The fact that she mentioned the Institutes. She knew how many there were. Which meant she probably knew what was happening in each one. Her father and the board had been keen that the Institutes on USA soil were nothing corruptible. To cure and contain more than kill. Never on your own doorstep was a familiar saying from her father. There was a part of Maria that wanted to say we can discuss the Institutes based here, Madam President. But you are not cleared for the others. This wasn't the time to show all her cards. Maria needed to be strong now. This was a battle the board had discussed quite frequently. Who was really running the country.

"No problem, Victoria, I look forward to it." They each took another drink. The silence continued. Neither woman wanted to really show their hand. Victoria was keen for her to know that at least she was now in the game.

"Shall we join the others, Maria? I am keen to show you my bowling skills." Victoria placed her glass down on the table.

"I would love to, Victoria. I will just drop this back in my room. Wouldn't want it falling into the wrong hands again. Would we?" Victoria heard exactly what Maria had said but it was her turn to not rise to the bait. They both left the study.

The president headed out to the bowling alley and Maria went back to the room. As soon as she entered, she placed the file on the bed and opened it. A quick glance told Maria that someone close to her had spoken. Given the president everything. This information was restricted to the main players only. It was all there the Brown Institute, the board, all of it. All of the Institutes, the weaponry, the technology, the research they had been doing. As a group they were light years ahead of anything that was on today's market, and now the president knew everything. Maria knew this was a leak from her board. Someone had changed sides. It was always a fear. If this person had changed sides and threw in with the president, then they had a plan to escape the eyes of the rest of the board. They must have cut a deal which included protection and immunity. Maria had a good idea who it was going to be. There was another board member at the table this evening. They never discussed or mentioned it when they are together but the fact that they are there was enough evidence that Maria needed. That wasn't for today though. Maria packed the file in her suitcase.

Maria's mind wandered to Damion. She didn't want him to be part of this. She was going to know from his reaction on her return. If they had played their cards together, Damion and the president, she was going to be able to tell. Reading people was a gift for Maria. Maria went back and joined them at the bowling. Damion was waiting for her on her return?

"Are you okay? Victoria has been here a while." He walked up and kissed her on the cheek as she entered.

"I am fine." Maria was looking him directly in the eye.

"Well, are you going to keep me in suspense? What did the boss want?" Maria kept his gaze. She knew he didn't know. That was a genuine question.

"To talk about the charity. It was only brief. Had to nip back to the room."

"Oh, okay, thought it might be something more exciting. So how is your bowling? Think we can take them down?" Damion escorted her to the lane.

"I am sure of it." Maria threw a glance at Victoria when she said that.

* * * *

They sat in the coffee shop watching the world go by. As she looked over at him she could tell that his wounds had healed. There were no visible scars. She knew there were still some there. under his suit, but he was so strong. One of the strongest men she had ever known. So protective. He was still hurting, but it wasn't going to keep him down. It wouldn't keep him from being next to her.

They knew what each other was thinking, as each person walked by. They smiled. They started playing a game. They each could tell if the person was good or bad. They started to gesture just for fun. Thumbs up and thumbs down. He was teasing her. Every now and again he would throw in a random thumbs down. At an old lady walking her dog. Or a vicar holding a Bible. It made her laugh. It was good to laugh. Food arrived from behind them. He tucked in. She wasn't hungry. She didn't seem to ever be hungry. The crowd was getting busier in front of them. He still played as he ate. They were having so much fun. Chris Masters walked past. It shocked her. She didn't expect to see Chris. Not here. Not now.

She looked over to him. He was still eating. It was brief but he was there. Her thumb was up. His was down. She couldn't tell if he was laughing at her or not. His mouth was full but his eyes said he was serious. His eyes said Chris was bad. When she turned to see Chris again, he as gone. Lost in the crowd. She carried on watching, expecting she may see him again. Dee Quaid appeared. She turned to him before making her opinion. She wanted to know what he thought. It was important, his answer was important to her. Had she lost her sense of opinion? He had his thumb down. She looked at her own thumb. As she did, he changed his and laughed. She changed hers. He had been teasing. Had he been teasing about Chris? Dee was lost in the shadows again. The night was drawing in. The guy across the road from them was getting out of a taxi. He was shouting at the taxi driver. He looked at her. She had her thumb up. So did he. It was Jack. It was Jack Quaid. She wanted to run over and talk to him. She had never had a real conversation with Jack but he disappeared into the crowd before she moved. It was Jack's dad's turn to make an appearance. He was walking slowly with a cane. She put her thumb up. He didn't, his thumb was down. Again, she couldn't work out his response. Was Jack's dad bad? What was he thinking? That he started this all? If he hadn't had Jack? He was still eating. She wished he had spoken. James Winters appeared. She was up again. He was down. He wasn't laughing. Did he not think these were good people? Were they bad people? She couldn't remember any more. She watched the crowd. The darker it became and the busier it was, the more she knew, the more she knew that they were still expecting someone. There was one person missing. It wouldn't be much longer until he arrived. She kept glancing over to him but he was still eating. She watched the crowd. He was there in the distance at first but he stood out. As if he was the only constant in a moving world around her. He was walking towards them. He kept walking towards them. She looked over at him still eating by her side smiling at her. She wanted to shout he was coming. Stop eating, he is coming. As she turned back, Michael was there. Standing in front of her. She was frozen to her seat. He stood fixated with her gaze. It got darker. It seemed like forever had passed. He didn't say a word to her. He moved his attention.

"Oliver, so good to see you again. Have you been looking after our girl?" Oliver stood up and shook Michael's hand.

"Yes, sir, just as you ordered. Keep close and all that. We are very, very close now, if you know what I mean?" Michael and Oliver laughed. They were friends, they were close. She could feel the chemistry off them.

"And what of the little quest? Is it still going on?"

"It is, sir. We may have had a short break but all is good. Can I order you something? I recommend the pasta, it is good." Michael sat down directly in front of Alex.

"Yes, why not? I hear the oysters here are amazing. How about some champagne and oysters? Let's celebrate. I hear we are going our separate ways soon, Alex? You are finally going to be rid of me? Yes, champagne and oysters, that is worth celebrating. Alex, does that sound good to you?" Alex didn't respond. She couldn't respond. Her voice didn't seem to work. Michael and Oliver were here together in person. Talking.

Joking. They were in this together. Was she in the way of them being together? Is that what this meant? Was it her that was the issue? Her mind was wandering in so many directions.

"Certainly, sir… How many would you like me to order?" Alex's head turned. Those words. Those words were there. Amongst those other words. How many?

"I don't know, Alex. How many, Alex?" She couldn't speak. The words wouldn't come out. Her throat was dry. There was so much she wanted to say but nothing was coming out.

"Alex, come, now, how many?" She didn't speak again.

"I think the cat has her tongue, Oliver, let me help you with that." As Michael said that, he picked the knife off the table.

"I said how many, Alex!" Michael plunged the knife into the front of Alex's neck.

Alex jumped up, she was grabbing at her throat as she did. Checking around her she could see she was in the back of the SUV. She had been murmuring in her sleep. While she was sleeping Oliver had explained everything to James. The side effects of the treatment, the need for the cure. He had agreed with James he would take Alex away once the cure was in place. The dreams were bad. As bad as Oliver had seen. James ignored her as she jumped. Oliver comforted her as he always did. They were heading to the hotel. The cure would be there this evening. This was the last night of dreams. Last night of the cravings, Oliver was convinced of it. After tomorrow they would be free of this. Free of Michael Mellor.

* * * *

"That will be breakfast, don't get up. We don't want you frightening the staff, do we?" Damion jumped out of bed and put on his dressing gown and fetched the tray from outside of the room. He brought it back to the bed. The chef had prepared them one of everything. And a dozen pancakes. Maria had made the mistake of telling Damion about breakfast with her mother and the energy. She was smiling as he brought the tray over.

"For energy, I am guessing." Maria sat up in bed.

"Yes, for energy. You are not as young as you used to be." She hit him in the arm as he said those words.

"Maria, are you okay? You seemed a little off after your conversation with Victoria last night. I thought you two got along?" Maria had been quiet. She had been working through her head all evening how to deal with the president. Victoria had played her hand. And being president of the United States it meant it was a hand with force. All evening she had smiled and been civil to her. But Maria knew the real reason for the continued eye contact. She wanted to know if she had shaken Maria. Maria didn't give anything away.

Maria and Damion had retired last. They spent a few hours lost in each other as soon as they were back in the room. Maria needed the distraction. Damion had that strong silent mode about him that made Maria feel protected and comfortable. He had held her as she slept through the night. As she woke this morning the president was back in her mind and how she was going to deal with the situation.

"I am fine, Damion. We are fine. I think we get on. She is a very powerful woman. Intimidating, some might say." Damion smiled.

"Only some might say. That is good though. Because I like you, Maria, and I want to spend as much time together as we can. Which means that we will be seeing more of Victoria." Maria knew that. She knew that whatever was to come she was going to have to take care of this situation with the president. Maybe bringing her in on this would make it legit. It was no longer about the money, the board had enough. Maria knew it was going to be more about how she could spin it as the future of their country. There would be a lot of dark secrets for the president to deal with. Once they were out there though they could move on. Maria could keep running the business with the president's backing. Which meant she would spend more time with Damion. It was slowly becoming her only way to get through this.

"Now, let's eat this and maybe go for a ride? The new stables are built and stocked with some beautiful animals. The helicopter isn't coming for us until this evening." She smiled back at him. Her mother was right. The president aside, she needed this. She needed to feel the normality of a relationship. Something real just for her. She gave him the nod to get rid of the tray. He didn't need telling twice. They were going to have to wait till lunch for something to eat. An hour and a half later they were at the stables.

"These horses are amazing. They must all be thoroughbred. To the highest pedigree." Maria stood stroking the neck of one of the six horses in the stables.

"I think they are. I am not a horse person. But when Victoria became president it was her one wish to have a Camp David. I didn't know you got this wish thing. Don't tell anyone though, I think it is a secret. Calms her down apparently. Riding horses, that is. Not having secrets." Maria wondered why she wasn't here this morning then. The president must be feeling the pressure as much as she was. If she had truly read all that information. Her head would have been buzzing with the empire that they had built over the last twenty years.

"So if you are to become president what would your one wish be to have at Camp David then, Damion?"

"You." There wasn't a second between the question and the answer. It was an instant reaction.

"You are so good at that. You should write a book on one-liners, you know that?" Maria was laughing as she spoke.

"I know, I am saving it for my memoirs. I think it could be a best-seller. I am never going to beat the girl in the red dress or Watergate. But you will be guaranteed a laugh at mine." Maria had no doubt it would be a best-seller and funny. He was a funny guy. Which you would have never got unless you were close to him. He had a face for every occasion.

"Seriously, what would be your one wish?" Damion was saddling his horse.

"A real shooting range. I have thought about it, even picked out where it will go. I do enjoy it. Targets, that is. I am not into this hunting lark. I know that is not going to go down well. But the only time you should shoot a living creature is in time of defence and war and then only if you really have to." This had surprised Maria. They had never discussed hunting.

221

She had presumed that due to his army days and his background he would be a fan.

"Another perfect answer. I would like that. I am an expert shot myself, don't you know? Club champion three years running. I will give you a run for your money, Mr Vice President." Christopher Mellor had enjoyed hunting. So had Michael. Maria never went with them unless it had been to the range. Christopher had hoped to change her mind but she never did. She did enjoy shooting targets as a way to release steam though.

"I remember. I went to that range too. Once or twice with your brother. He was quite the shot too. But always bragged about you. His cool twin sister. So I look forward to the challenge, Miss Mellor." She hadn't known that. She didn't realise that him and Michael had spent that much time together. It was nice. It was nice that he remembered Michael. Every time he spoke of Michael it had been with fondness. They would have been best friends if Michael hadn't have had his condition, she was sure of it.

"So you don't really ride then? If you are not a horse person?" Maria was keen to explore more about him.

"Oh, I ride. I wouldn't say well, but I can ride."

"Something that you don't do well? Now that is something I can't wait to see. So far you have been…" Maria stopped herself at that point. She was about to say perfect at everything. Her guard had dropped for a moment.

"Average, fair to average. So poor is good to see." Damion knew what she had meant. He also knew what she was about to say. He had been throwing his A game at her since they met.

"I think she chose a lovely spot here, to be able to see all of Camp David. Well, most of it." Damion walked Maria over to the entrance of the stables. They stood and looked at the view. He had his arm around her. It felt nice.

"I never thought I would be here, you know. There were times when I was in Iraq that I worried about getting through the day, let alone being vice president of the United States." Damion was sounding very melancholy. This was the softer, more vulnerable side of him coming out.

"You have achieved so much. You should be proud of yourself." She turned and kissed him on the cheek. It felt like the right thing to do. Everyone needed reassurance at some point.

"Look who is saying that. I think what you achieved is amazing. Losing your father and your brother and still taking over the business. Running the company. I don't know what I would have done without my father. Or my uncle, for that point. They have believed in me from day one. Even when I didn't believe in myself." Maria was looking at him now. There was a connection between them. They had shared so much. Her father had been exactly the same. He had been the person building her to take over the business even though she didn't see it. Her mother had done the same. Steering her. Ensuring she knew all the right contacts. They were children of powerful people and their parents had wanted the best for them.

"I know how that feels. My mum and dad. The more I look at this now, the more I understand how they have helped shape me to be where I am today." He smiled directly at her and leaned in and kissed her. The kiss was real. There was a

223

giving in those lips as if it was the first time and lasted like it was the last time. Kissing was something Maria had missed, and now to be kissed like that had her weak at the knees. He stopped kissing her. She could breathe again.

"They should be so proud of you, Maria. You are doing an amazing job." That felt good to hear.

"Now that you are head of the board I know you are going to do remarkable things in the next few years." She smiled. That is exactly what she thought.

"Thank you." As the words left her mouth she knew something was wrong. He had just said the board. He didn't know about the board. The thought ran slow motion through her brain. He knew, he knows.

That was as much as Maria had time to think about it. It wasn't an accident that he said it. He just wanted her to know. There was something deep down in Damion that made him want to show people he had control. He was always in control. Something that meant he could turn on the charm as quickly as he could turn on the rage.

In Iraq he had the most successful kills in his division, he was a decorated war hero. He killed people and they put medals on his chest for doing so. He didn't do it for the medals. He did it because he enjoyed it. He was good at it. It almost felt to him like he was born to do it.

Damion had a horseshoe still in his hand and knocked Maria unconscious. As she fell he caught her with his other hand. She was out cold. He dragged her over to the haystack in the corner. He laid her gently into the hay. As she lay there he leaned in and kissed her. He mouthed the words "thank you" to her. He then climbed to the top of the pile and pulled down a blanket. He placed it next to Maria and unwrapped it. It was a high powered rifle. With ease he set it up at the window. He had done this a thousand times in training. He aimed the sight and waited. He knew the timing was good. He had been watching the time all the time that he was pretending to fix his saddle. He had a copy of the president's schedule at all times, and he knew she was leaving earlier than them. Two minutes later the president stepped out of her quarters with her husband. Damion aimed the rifle. With two shots he was now in line to be the next president of the United States. Victoria and her husband were both dead. With speed he turned and placed the gun in Maria's hand, firing a third shot into the haystack. Damion Charles was out the back of the stables and heading back to the guest quarters before the secret service knew what was going on.

Chapter 12

Alex laid on the sofa in the hotel suite. She was in and out of reality, trying to keep in touch with everything that was going on around her.

"They will be here shortly, Oliver. Just be patient." She could tell that Oliver was concerned. It was in his voice. She had heard it often over the last few months. He had been hovering over her for at least an hour.

She could feel the sweat pouring down her face as she laid there. Oliver had been using a damp cloth on her forehead to try and cool her down. The more she resisted the urges, the hotter her body would become.

James was cool. It was almost as if Alex could see a cold bubble around him. He didn't seem to be worried about anything. That worried Alex. She didn't like James. The words continued around her. Four men as far as she could tell all talking. It wasn't about her. It was all about the Mellors. The Foundation. The cure. They each had a story. They had each seen something the other had not. It was the key to the Mellor Foundation. Key to the Mellors. They segregated everything, even the staff. They took a different member of staff to each

Institute. Oliver knew a lot about the Brown Institute. He was their man. Their man that had supported the Mellors. Adrian, Adrian had been to China. He had spent a lot of time in China with Christopher Mellor. Alex could make out some of the conversation. It was around control. Control of governments. Control of money markets. They had the technology to control all of it. The third guy. Not James. Alex didn't pick up on his name but he was weapons. Military weapons. She was sure that was what he was saying. He had been to Groom Lake. Nevada. That is their Institute. The second Institute in the USA. Alex was trying to remember that at all times. There were two Institutes here. That was important. The cure was coming from one of them. This man, he knew stuff. Stuff other people weren't allowed to talk about. Alex was getting confused with his conversation. He had been fifty-one. He didn't look fifty-one but he was sure about it. She tried to drown out the conversation just to hear Oliver's voice. It was hard, but it was a voice that she trusted. It was all she trusted.

She knew why she was there. She was there for all this to end. That is what she had wanted. It is what they both had wanted. They wanted a normal life. Oliver was good for her. Their time together had shown that. He looked after her. He was always there for her. He had been strong for her even when she couldn't be strong for herself. She could trust him with everything. She did trust him with everything. This was his idea. This was his idea? He had decided this?

But the dream. She couldn't forget the last dream she had. Alex was confused by the message. What was it telling her? Was her subconscious telling her something different? Oliver didn't share her opinions. He didn't know right from wrong?

Should she really trust him? She hadn't expected that. Was he right and she was wrong? She couldn't trust herself at the moment. Could she really trust him? He knew Michael?

She knew she had been doctored at the Institute. Oliver hadn't. Did Oliver know better than her? Ever since the dream that was all she was able to think about. He lifted her head and gave her some water. She took it and swallowed it. As she swallowed, she feared it was poison. If she had the energy she would have run to the bathroom and thrown up. But she didn't. She couldn't move. He was smiling at her. She couldn't tell if it was a real smile or a fake one. Was he as in to the relationship as her? Was he invested into her? She started to doubt him. Was he just keeping an eye on her? That's how it had started. That's what Michael had said. Are you looking after our girl? Was this all a game? Was she alone in this? Did she even need him? She wasn't alone in this, she knew it. He was always here. He was going to be with her to the end. That was for sure.

There were more people in the room now. Three more. She hadn't noticed them coming in. She had an urge to jump up and speak with them. Deal with them. What were they there for? Were they there for her? There was conversation, but the words were disappearing even quicker than they spoke them. She couldn't make it out. The three men that entered the room, they were talking to Oliver and James and the other two guys. The other two guys left. Two of the three new guys left. There was only four of them in the room. Those three and her. They were still talking. She could hear them. They were talking about her. She could make out her name. Over and over again she heard her name. They were worried. They were worried for her, she was sure of it. The room stopped. It stopped still, not a movement. Everyone froze in front of her. He was there. It was why the room had frozen. He was there with her. She spotted him by the door. He walked across the room. Nobody else could see him. He lifted her and sat her up on the sofa. He knelt before her. Holding her hand.

"Are you okay, Alex?" She nodded her head. She wanted to speak but couldn't. She wanted to tell Oliver he was here. Here in the room.

"Look at me, Alex. Look me in the eyes. I have something serious to tell you." Alex did. Those eyes had mesmerised her for so long. There was nowhere else she was going to look.

"They want to change you, Alex. They don't believe in you. They don't believe in your cause. I believe in you, Alex. I have always believed in you. We started this journey together... Think of all the good you have done? Think of everything you have achieved. How many people in this world are safe because of you? Hundreds, Alex, hundreds." Alex knew this to be true, he spoke the truth. She had saved them all. That is what she was trying to do. Was he really the only one that believed in her? He was there. He had been there nearly every night with her.

The scene behind her began to move, slowly at first but they were catching up with her and Michael. Everything was coming into focus.

"Is that what you want, Alex? Do you want to go back to the Alex you were a year ago? At your desk with James? Looking after traffic? Is that what you really want?" She was shaking her head. She remembered the heartache. She knew how lonely she was. The endless nights alone. She hadn't been alone for months. They were always with her.

"But I am broken?" The words fell out of her lips. She hadn't meant them to. The other words hadn't been able to get out. But those ones did.

"Who says you are broken, Alex? They said so? So you have held yourself back? You are not broken, Alex? You are finally you. You are who you are meant to be, Alex." Alex was confused.

"The Brown Institute?" Her voice was coming back to her. Michael was smiling at her. He was rubbing her hand. It felt nice.

"Our home? It is where we began, Alex. They didn't do anything to us. We were already these people. They just helped us realise it. Before we were alone. We were always alone. Now we have a family. A family that is the same as us. We are family, Alex." The more Michael spoke, the more he made sense to her. She wanted to trust him but he wasn't who she trusted. Oliver kept flashing in her head. He was who she trusted. But he was ignoring them. Ignoring Michael. She could see him talking to the stranger and James. Paying her no attention. Was he under orders? Was he under Michael's orders?

"You can't trust them, Alex." She kept thinking of the dreams. Were they telling her not to trust Oliver? He wasn't going to be there in the end. Michael was. Michael was always going to be there. He was her partner in this. Wasn't he?

James was there. She knew she didn't trust James. He wanted to kill her. He wanted Oliver back. They were friends, it had nothing to do with her. What if that was it? What if this didn't work? What if James had brought someone here to kill her? That would solve everything. He would have Oliver back. It wouldn't be his fault. It would be the stranger's. Alex was trying to focus. They had it. They were preparing it. The injection was going to kill her. James wanted her dead. He was a killer. Michael was still there but he had blended into the background. Against the wall. He was quiet now and just stood watching. Alex looked around the room. Oliver's gun was on the side next to the sofa. She jumped for it. Before anyone could move she had it straight out in front of her.

"Stop!" Everyone turned to face Alex.

"Alex, what are you doing?" Oliver started to walk towards her.

"Stop where you are." Oliver froze.

"Alex, you are not well, put the gun down and let us help you. We have the cure, Alex, this is it." Oliver was holding it in his hand.

"I am not taking it. I am not taking the poison. This is all a plan to get rid of me?" Alex's hands were shaking in front of her. She was looking at Michael for confirmation. He was nodding at her. They could see she was looking into the corner. Oliver was worried. He knew there was always someone in her dream with her.

"This is really none of my…" The stranger started to head towards the door. Alex shot him. He fell to the ground. It was a head shot. The silencer on the gun had been a blessing to them all that it didn't raise the attention of the people in the hotel.

"Alex, what the fuck are you doing?" James was now shouting at her. Alex was moving the gun between James and Oliver.

"He was here to kill me. The same as you, James. You want me dead. You want Oliver back. Back before he met me." James was now looking at Oliver. They needed a distraction to take her down. They needed to rush her and put her on the floor. Oliver had the cure in his hand. The doctor had already said his goodbyes before Alex jumped off the sofa.

Chris Masters appeared between James and Oliver. He was there in the room with them. Alex started to panic. She could see him. She could see Michael. Something was wrong. This can't be real.

"Listen to him, Alex." Michael was whispering to her. She could hear him. He didn't move from the wall but she knew it was his voice.

"He killed me, Alex. He killed me. I only wanted the best for you. He killed James too. Drove up next to him and shot him in his car." Alex was watching the blood pour down Chris' face. He didn't deserve to die. He was a good man. He loved her. They were killing the people she loved.

"You killed him. You killed my partner. He did nothing to you." Alex was waving the gun at James.

"Alex, I didn't kill anyone? I didn't kill your partner." James was looking at Oliver again.

"You did. You killed him. And you killed James. You want to kill me now. Who is next? My Family? My brother? My mother? Who is next? My friends, my friend Dee?" James looked at the floor. Michael was whispering again.

"Did you see that, Alex? Did you see him look down? She is dead already. They are dead already. When was the last time you saw them? Do you know if any of them are still alive? What have they been doing while you were saving people?" Alex steadied her hand. Oliver could tell what was coming.

"Alex, Alex, concentrate. Concentrate on me. James didn't kill anyone. I killed Chris, Alex. I killed James too. It had nothing to do with James. They were the orders, Alex. They had a copy of the hard drive. It was too dangerous. Too dangerous for you. I did that for you, Alex. You know that. You know deep down inside that everything I do is for you. For us. You know that don't you, Alex? If that was out there, then they would have all been taken care of. Your family would have been next. Christopher Mellor would have made sure of it, Alex. But I took care of it, Alex. For us. For our future." Alex moved the gun towards Oliver.

"You killed them? You killed my colleagues. My friends." Oliver was walking towards her.

"For you, Alex, to save you. I would kill anyone." As Oliver's last word came out, the whisper from Michael was in the other ear.

"Did you hear that, Alex? Anyone. Anyone you love. How many people do you think he would kill for you, Alex, how many?" Those words were always followed by the same action. Three bullets put an end to the conversation. Before James could move, the gun was back pointing at him.

"My family. My family, James, are they alive?" James nodded. Even as ex-forces he was shocked that she had just shot Oliver in front of him. Oliver had been everything to her. She had meant everything to him.

"What about your friend, Alex?" The whisper was there again. He was next to her now. She could feel his breath on her neck.

"Dee. Dee is okay too?" James was nodding to say she was okay.

"Liar." Alex didn't know where the word came from. Was it her or Michael? It only took two bullets to end James. He had hit Alex for the last time. Alex walked over to Oliver and took the syringe from his hand. She placed it on the floor and stepped on it until it broke. The liquid bled into the carpet.

"Shall we go, Alex?" Michael stood next to her. She picked up her jacket off the chair and put it on. Michael opened the door and let her out first. Alex stepped into the hallway. Darkness fell...